LUST

LUST

EROTIC FANTASIES FOR WOMEN

EDITED BY
VIOLET BLUE

CLEIS
PRESS

Published in the United States by
Cleis Press Inc., P.O. Box 14697, San Francisco, California 94114.

Printed in the United States.
Cover design: Scott Idleman
Cover photograph: Samantha Wolov
Text design: Frank Wiedemann
Cleis Press logo art: Juana Alicia
First Edition.
10 9 8 7 6

Acknowledgments

Love, admiration and a toast to the future go to Frédérique Delacoste and Felice Newman; our relationships mean more than I can express here. My deepest feelings are reserved for my family—Survival Research Laboratories and Mark Pauline. My love: Jonathan.

Contents

INTRODUCTION: THE ART OF HUNGER

This collection of explicit erotic fiction by women has been titled *Lust*. That's a short, simple name and at first glance it could seem like a very self-aggrandizing title for a single book. It is after all a concept that has filled volumes; its urgency has destroyed hearts, minds and empires; its complexity rules us in ways we'd sometimes rather not explore—yet want to, oh so badly. That's why *Lust* is a perfect title for the stories between these pages. Each one captures the uncontrollable, draws it out, and we get to savor every act of irresistible hunger, desire and the point of no return: lust.

When lust overcomes you, you barely know who you are or what you are doing. Each of the women in the following selections knows this feeling, and the skilled authors represented here—both new and well known—faithfully capture that feeling in each woman's passage from ordinary to extraordinary sexual hunger.

For instance: In K. L. Gillespie's "Golden Hand," a slick pickpocket gets far more than she bargained for in a chance, anonymous encounter on a crowded train. When desire trumps theft, she has no choice but to submit to it. In "Ripe Fruit," Bonnie Dee gives us a truly heated taste of both the pleasures of impulse sex and the creative use of summertime fruits. Being overcome with lust is hard work for some—especially the female private investigator in Teresa Noelle Roberts' "Sixth Sense," whose investigation goes from routine to highly unprofessional when she takes total control of the situation. Kay Jaybee's "Tied to the Kitchen Sink" is a playful and randily inspiring tale of casual lust that'll have you thinking differently about both birthday presents and housework.

Lust makes the real surreal, and changes our boundaries when we're in its heat. As happens in "The Butch, the Boy and Me," by Andrea Zanin, in which a butch dyke stretches her sexual orientation a bit to try on a man and a very happy female enabler. Sloane Square's "The Hall of Justice" takes the three-way into another, less controllable direction when a public hookup among costumed club-goers goes all the way, and then some. Saskia Walker's sexy, stylized skills excel in "The Importance of Good Networking," making office life into the hotbed of unbridled lust and sexy IT nerds we've always dreamed about.

"Coffee Shop Boy," by A. D. R. Forte, builds tension to the breaking point in that classic scenario—lusting after the hot guy you see every day at the coffee shop—but the female forensic scientist in the starring role has a very different method of turning him into her toy. Geneva King's "American Bottom in Limousin" will surprise even those readers with the dirtiest jail fantasies, as a girl finds herself behind bars in a foreign country and is offered a tense deal for release. "Pleasant Surprise," by Maria Grigoriadis, is a surprise that isn't merely pleasant, but downright incendiary—when a sexy stranger shows up at her door, shushing her and asking for a hot fuck, what else can the girl do?

Susan St. Aubin's beautiful, lyrical "Moving" is a long, lusty stroll (literally) for a woman who thinks she's past all that lust stuff until a heckler she walks by every day gets her to slow down and rediscover skin, sex, heat and the desire she thought she'd outgrown. "Out of the Shower," by Maria Matthews, portrays the ultimate in instant, freshly washed lust: a woman steps from the tub and right into a blindfold and some delicious light pain, bondage and sexual submission to the man who loves her.

"Love Triangle," by B. J. Franklin, offers us a girl so over-come with lust that she gets caught watching her male lust object get off—and you won't believe what *his* boyfriend does. Jean Roberta's "Het Cats" isn't just a playful turn across the LGBT dance floor, but a line-crossing tale of tear-each-other's-clothes-off sex between two very unlikely people. A darker, yet wholly consuming and arousing turn is Debra Hyde's "Kidnapped," which delivers exactly what the title implies: rough sex, and more. After a hot nonconsensual fantasy, how about some shop-ping lust? Kristina Wright's "Satisfaction Guaranteed" takes us into the fantasyland behind closed doors in a sex shop, where the manager is as ready as the toys to make the customers happy. And finally, Reen Guierre takes lust on a river adventure and a young woman drifts into a spontaneous, riveting and unex-pected tryst while "Tubing the Brule."

I hope that you find as much good friction in these stories as the women inhabiting them. A book about swimming may not save anyone from drowning, but my hope is that *Lust* will make you hungry enough to perform more than a few acts of lust. For satisfaction, for desire, for love; even without an audience, the hunger artist must perform. Kafka got that part right, anyway.

Violet Blue
April 2007

GOLDEN HAND

K. L. Gillespie

It had started out just like any other Friday. Rush hour was well under way and Molly Frith had already picked two pockets by the time she arrived at Victoria Station. She worked the main concourse for twenty minutes or so before jumping into a black cab and heading over to the City, where the richest pickings were to be had. She always took taxis, unless she was following a mark, because the public transport system was full of criminals.

Molly had been dipping professionally in her own inimitable way since she was fifteen, and she had it down to a fine art. She had honed her skills on the Paris Metro, where she was known locally as "la main d'or," until she had her heart broken by a French Lothario and moved back to London.

Meanwhile, south of the river, Nicholas Sackworth was running late. He had slept in for the second time that week and he had an important meeting at ten that he hadn't even begun preparing for. He was also suffering from a splitting headache caused by one too many tequilas the night before and he wasn't sure, because his memory hadn't sobered up yet, but he thought he might have argued with his wife at some point in the last twelve hours because when he woke up this morning he was on the sofa. Despite his thundering migraine he had to run for his train and only just managed to slip through the automatic doors as they were beeping shut. There were no seats left so he leaned against the glass partition and closed his eyes while the train cut through South London toward the City.

While Molly was speeding along the Embankment in the back of a hackney cab she was already planning the rest of her day. Brunch with girlfriends at the Ivy, shopping at Harvey Nichols for a new outfit and a gallery opening at seven for yet another Young Brilliant Artist. It was a lot to fit in and unbeknown to her society friends, it was all paid for by crime. She didn't look like a pickpocket. Her clothes, amongst other things, reeked of money; they had to, they were a tool of the trade and they allowed her to melt seamlessly into the crowds of commuters that she worked five days a week. They were also her get-out-of-jail card because on the rare occasion that she did get caught, what overworked, stressed-out, ex–public school boy could resist her raven-black hair, five-inch Louboutins and custom-made, seamed stockings. None so far, that's for sure.

Nicholas spent his fifteen-minute journey, as usual, drifting in and out of a waking dream in which he was tied to a bed by a beautiful woman, naked but for silk stockings and stilettos, who explored his body at her whim. It was only when the train pulled into the station and the doors jolted open that he woke up with a start. His dream was long gone but a throbbing erection in his pants was still there to remind him.

Against his will he was herded onto the platform by a wave of commuters, his hard-on still burning into his hip and work the last thing on his mind, until he caught sight of the time and the real world came crashing down on him. He still hadn't prepared for his meeting and he was still running late. His erection subsided and he desperately wanted a cigarette so as soon as he was through the barriers he headed to the nearest shop and bought ten Marlboro. A tinge of guilt hit him, but his wife would never know and he could always give up again tomorrow.

London Bridge was still heaving when Molly arrived, just the way she liked it: overcrowded and anonymous, perfect pick-pocketing territory, and popular too. Molly had already spotted three other run-of-the-mill dippers working the crowds, hiding their intent behind a folded jacket or unread newspaper. They stood out like sore thumbs and she knew the police would be watching them so for her own good she moved to the other side of the station, positioned herself under the announcement board and kept her eyes peeled.

Nicholas lit a cigarette on his way out of the shop. It was his first of the day and he savored every drag. It was the fags that he had argued with his wife about last night. Something about sperm counts and starting a family. This last bit made him laugh because they would have to be fucking to start a family and they hadn't done that in weeks. And it was nothing to do with smoking or sperm counts, it was her constant bickering that was putting him off and it wasn't a nicotine patch he needed, it was a scold's bridle to shut her up. They'd only been married two years and both of them knew they'd settled for each other out of desperation because the inevitable onslaught of the big four-oh was bearing down on them and all their friends were married.

Then, by a process of elimination, they'd ended up sitting to-gether at some party and the next thing he knew they were en-gaged, then they were married and now she wanted a baby and he had no idea how he'd gotten stuck in such a big rut. Nicholas took a rebellious drag of his cigarette and drew the comforting smoke deep down into his lungs.

Molly scanned the station and within seconds she had found her mark. He was standing at the nape of the escalators hungrily smoking a cigarette and experience told her that he had other things on his mind and would be an easy lift. He was tall, in his midthirties and well dressed, just Molly's type. She watched his every move with the eyes of a hunter.

Nicholas checked his watch out of habit, time was getting on so he threw his cigarette butt away and headed into the tube.

When Molly saw him disappear into the underground she knew she had picked well. Instinct told her to follow him but she had to move fast so she trotted across the station in her spike-heeled Louboutins, stepping over his discarded dog end, and tailgated him down the escalator.

That morning's argument with his wife was beginning to come back to Nicholas and it all sounded so familiar. He knew hav-ing a baby would be a big mistake and he knew his wife only wanted one to fill the gap left by the job she gave up when they got married. He knew something else, too: he didn't love her and they had nothing in common; that thought swam round and round his head as the escalator plunged him deeper into the tube network.

Molly followed him down into the surreal depths of the Northern Line, thanking her lucky stars that he had bypassed the Jubilee Line because there were far too many security cameras on that platform for comfort. A sea of heads stretched out in front of her but she was focused and never lost sight of his dark brown hair bobbing above the crowd. She felt at home weaving through the subterranean network of tunnels that connected London. The tube had always been her favorite hunting ground; it did half the work for you because people expected to be bustled and pushed up against, especially in rush hour, so her deft hand could easily go unnoticed as it slipped in and out of unsuspecting men's pockets.

Nicholas squeezed through the crowds banking up on the northbound platform and waited. He should have used the downtime to go through his notes for the meeting but fleeting images of the girl in stockings and hard-core bondage kept infiltrating his mind's eye and he couldn't concentrate on anything else. His cock was stirring in his pants again and he threw willpower to the wind and let the fanciful femme have her wicked way with him for the second time that day.

As Molly entered the platform a train pulled in and she only just managed to squeeze into the carriage behind her mark. She fanned him without anyone noticing and decided that his wallet could be in either of his two front trouser pockets, both were carrying something of comparable size and she had a fifty-fifty chance of entering the right pocket first time.

The doors closed and as the carriage jerked off she tipped forward onto her toes and jutted her breasts into his back. She felt his feet adjust, strengthening his balance and he leaned back into her, increasing the pressure between her nipples and his shoulder blades. First contact had been made and in five seconds he would be used to the pressure of her body against his.

Nicholas was oblivious to the young woman pressing up against him; the tube was always overcrowded and he was used to being jostled every morning. Besides, by that point his fantasy was in full swing and he was too busy wishing he was somewhere else, somewhere private where he could give his erection the attention it demanded, to notice anything happening around him.

As they entered the tunnel and darkness swamped the train Molly's hand entered his left trouser pocket. Her touch was light, the lightest, and she was sure that he hadn't felt a thing. She had expected her polished, carmine fingertips to find his wallet straightaway and whip it in a split second but she was momentarily thrown when they rested on his erect penis. She knew she had to stay professional, but his cock was throbbing hypnotically beneath her fingertips and there was no way that he could have failed to notice her hand cupping the tip of his erection. Still, he hadn't even flinched.

Nicholas had noticed, but the shock of feeling someone else's fingers on him—on the tube, at twenty past nine in the morning—made him freeze. He knew he should have turned round and demanded to know what was going on but something was stopping him. The touch was so charged his blood ran through his veins like electricity and he succumbed completely to her touch.

When Molly sensed his submission it set her pulse racing; when she gently squeezed him and his breathing deepened she realized that she had complete control. With this free rein Molly started to run her nails over his cock. The lining of his trousers was as thin as silk and she could feel every ridge and vein as she probed deeper and deeper into his pocket.

Molly had him in the palm of her hand and she basked in the sense of power it gave her. She could feel her cunt throbbing against the lace of her pants and she squeezed her thighs together, putting gentle pressure on her vulva. The rocking of the carriage masked her movement as she worked her hand up and down the length of his cock. She allowed her blood-red nails to play over the marshmallow softness of his glans as it strained against his trousers and she dragged at the inside of his pocket with her expensive manicure, desperate to feel his naked flesh.

Nicholas badly wanted to see who was touching him so exquisitely but he was scared that if he turned round it would stop and she would disappear into thin air. Eventually, unable to resist, he strained his eyes to the side as far as he could without moving his neck and caught a glimpse of her shoes and stockings reflected in the door. It was enough to send his libido hurtling into orbit and he lifted his briefcase to waist height, providing her with a shield to work behind as she pushed his foreskin to and fro with relish.

Molly pulled him toward her and picked up the pace. She pushed herself into his back and parted her legs, forcing her pudendum into his gyrating arse as it buffeted backward and forward. She gritted her teeth and wave after wave of unrestrained pleasure started to swamp her body as she hungrily allowed her other hand to wander round his waist and over his taut torso.

Nicholas could feel her thrusting against him and the more she thrust the more disengaged he became with the world around him. His heart was pounding against his chest and he continued moving with her, swaying his hips in time with her strokes while rapid, rhythmic contractions swirled round the base of his penis and his pelvis jerked. He had reached inevitability and there was no going back now.

Molly was unable to control herself any longer and she slipped her fingers down the waistband of her skirt and cupped her cunt tightly in her hand. She was already slick and needed only the slightest bit of pressure, expertly applied, to tease out an orgasm. She came easily, without batting an eyelid or missing a stroke and as the train rushed through the tunnel her mark hurtled toward his orgasm.

Nicholas felt his whole body tense in anticipation and lost himself in the moment. The last thing he remembered before he was thrown into the vortex of his own climax was her body spasming against his, and as the train pulled into the station he came, and came, and came.

Molly felt his warm come seeping through his pocket as his cock went limp and she silently withdrew her hand. The train came to a standstill and Molly slipped out quietly. She knew from experience that it would have been awkward otherwise, and anyway, what else could she have done? Introduce herself, make small talk, exchange phone numbers? No, she was sure she had done the right thing.

Spent, it took Nicholas a moment to compose himself. Part of him felt cheap and abused but his heart was pounding and his mind was racing. He couldn't make sense of anything that had happened but it had been exhilarating and he was hooked. He wanted more: to follow her, to thank her, to see her again per-haps, but she had already disappeared into the crowds and he knew it was over.

Molly opened her bag on the escalator and took the wallet out: black leather, soft, expensive. She stroked it before opening it up and taking out his Visa card. Nicholas Sackworth, he had a name now. There was a photo too and for some reason she couldn't put it down. She stared at it all the way up the escalator, memorizing his face, desperately looking for clues to his life, but it was just a passport photo and the orange backdrop told her nothing. Nevertheless, she kept it along with the eighty quid that she had found but threw the rest away in the nearest bin before stepping into the road and hailing a taxi.

RIPE FRUIT

Bonnie Dee

Hot! It is ninety-some degrees and my cabbages are wilting. My corn leaves look dry and brown instead of lush and green. The raspberries are ripening into a soupy mash in their little boxes. If I fermented them I could probably make wine. The rich, fruity smell of melons and peaches combined with the stifling heat is making me nauseous. If I never see, smell or ingest another fruit or vegetable in my life it will be too soon.

A car blows by on the road raising a cloud of dust, choking me with exhaust fumes and dry earth. Looking down at "A Carol of Harvest for 1867," I try to concentrate on Whitman's lyrical eloquence about nature instead of the mundane reality of it that surrounds me. It's obvious Whitman never had to run a produce stand or he wouldn't have waxed poetic about the green stuff.

Bored! I have this *Leaves of Grass* thing to read and a paper to write about it. Then I have a psych test to study for but I can't concentrate. It's far too hot and I have a headache. I want air-conditioning, a bottle of beer and some mindless MTV reality show. My needs are reduced to just that.

If sweat wasn't trickling down my spine and sticking my shirt to my breasts, I might have the energy to entertain myself here in my plywood shanty. Other days, when the customers were few and far between, I'd spent some time getting to know the vegetables. Cucumbers became my special friends. I would take one behind the cash register counter and introduce it to my pussy while I fantasized a hot, summer stud. It's not as satisfying as the real deal but one makes do in a wasteland.

Today I look at the limp, sad cukes and let them rest. I lay my book on the counter, my head on the book, and rest too. My cheek sticks to my arm and my eyelids drift closed, probably to seal shut forever with sweat.

Ninety-some degrees. No one wants vegetables. No sane person would venture out of the house or the swimming pool on such a day. I rebuke myself for conjuring images of a pool and water—cold, clear, beautiful water. I dream of splashing in it, diving and surfacing, watching the sun glitter across the dancing wavelets.

Beneath the water, something grabs my leg and tugs me under. I gulp for air and then go down but I'm not afraid. When my head bobs to the surface again, someone is there with me. His hair is black and slick as a seal's. His eyelashes shed water as he blinks and grins at me, showing even white teeth. Tan shoulders break the water and his rocky chest is like an island floating in the pool.

"Hey there, Pool Boy. Come clean my filter." I feel his hand touching me under the water, a finger slipping into the waistband of my bathing suit and delving lower....

"Excuse me, miss?"

I snap awake and sit up straight so fast that I almost fall backward off the stool. "Yes?"

"I want to buy a peach."

I look up and am blind for a moment. The man is backlit against the bright sunlight. He is only a dark silhouette and for a moment I think he looks exactly like the pool boy in my dream. I blink and resist the urge to rub my eyes with my fists like a child waking from a nap. "Of course. Um, we have half-peck bags or a full peck. If you want them for canning, you can buy a whole bushel."

"No. I only want one peach."

The guy steps out of the light and I stand and move around the counter. Now I can see his face. He doesn't look like the hot pool boy in my dream. He looks even better.

I take in his wavy black hair, dark eyes, arched brows, sculpted cheekbones and full-lipped mouth. He has one of those mouths with the deep bow in the upper lip and a sexy lower one you'd like to bite a chunk out of. I look past him to his car, low-slung, sleek, jet black and shiny. This guy is money.

His face is vaguely familiar and I'm thinking that I should recognize him. Maybe he's a minor celebrity of some type, a singer, actor or model that I've seen in a magazine or on a TV screen.

"Just one peach." I smile. "Go ahead and pick one."

"I didn't know if I could buy only one or if you just sell them by the bag."

I'm tempted to tell him, yes, he does need to buy a bag, because I haven't sold anything all afternoon. Instead I smile even wider and say, "No. One is fine. I'll charge you a quarter. Does that sound fair?"

"I don't think it'll break me." He grins back at me and he's adorable. He scratches the side of his neck with one hand and looks from me to the table of produce. "The problem is I don't know how to tell what's ripe."

I'm not about to explain that everything on that table has

been ripened to mush from the hot weather. I sashay over to the peaches with an extra swing to my hips and select one of the firmer fruits. I present it to him, pressing it slightly with my fingers.

"Here. Feel this." I place it on his palm and it looks tiny in his big hand. "Give it a little squeeze. Not too hard, not too soft, see? It should be good and juicy and sweet." I don't mean to make the words suggestive but they sit there, resonating with double meaning all on their own.

I look up into his eyes and he's not looking at the peach in his hand but at my cleavage. His tongue darts out, licking his lips.

"Go ahead and try it," I say and I *do* mean to sound suggestive this time.

Ten minutes earlier I'd felt about as sexy as a garden slug. My pits were sweating, my hair was limp and a slick of oil shone on my face. Now, suddenly I feel like Eve offering the apple. I am sex personified. One of the straps of my tank top slips provocatively down my shoulder like I'm a Dogpatch slut. This guy radiates magnetism and my crotch clenches and unclenches under siege from a sharp surge of lust.

The pretty man bites into the fruit with his white teeth. His eyes never leave mine as the ripe fruit bursts into his mouth, releasing thick, honeyed juice. A little trickles from the corner of his mouth and I unconsciously run my tongue out to the side of my own mouth as if to catch it.

"Good?"

He nods, chewing and swallowing. "Nectar." He wipes the sticky juice from his face with the back of his hand and extends the peach toward me. "Want a bite?"

I completely forget that I've sworn off fruit for life, that the very smell of it gives me a headache now, that the only good peach is a dead peach. I take the fruit from his outstretched hand

and bite into it. Of course, he's right. It *is* sweet nectar in my mouth. The taste of a peach perfectly reflects its bright golden-red color. It tastes exactly the way it should.

Despite sucking in as I bite, some of the juice escapes my mouth and wets my chin. When I pull the peach away from my lips, the man reaches out to wipe my chin with his finger then sucks the juice from it. I watch entranced as the finger enters his mouth, his cheeks hollow with sucking. I hear the firm pop his lips make when he takes it back out. My own lips purse, half-parted in anticipation.

He leans in and I meet him halfway, hypnotized. Our lips touch and we kiss. His tongue parts my lips and sweeps inside my mouth to taste me. We don't touch anywhere except our lips. My pussy swells like an overripe peach ready to burst.

His mouth drops lower to lick my chin clean of the sticky residue of juice and then he pulls back. "You taste like summer," he says with a smile. "Salty and sweet."

My pulse pounds. I'm ready for more. I dismiss the fact that the day is hotter than the sun's surface. I'm anxious to sweat some more with this stranger.

"Look, do you want to sit in my car for a while and get cooled off?" he asks.

The idea of sitting in cushioned, air-conditioned comfort and making out with this hot guy sounds like heaven, but I'm cautious.

"My mother warned me about getting into strangers' cars," I say with a laugh, fingering the peach, which is still dripping in my hand.

"But I'm not really a stranger."

There's a pause during which he looks at me expectantly, then an almost comical look of dismay comes over his face when it's clear that I don't know who he is.

"I'm Tom Stander. I play Bobby on 'Wild Hearts.' "

"*Oh,*" I exclaim. "That show. Yeah. Sorry. I don't really watch soaps."

"Oh." The word is small. It's obviously been a long time since Tom has interacted with anyone except adoring fans.

"Rachel Neidema." I supply my name and hold his peach back toward him. "And even actors can be serial killers."

"But, I'm not. I swear." The twinkle has returned and the way it dances across his dark eyes reminds me of my pool dream. "I have an idea. Why don't you help me pick out some more ripe fruit—a melon and a box of berries. We can take it to my hotel room and have a picnic."

I hesitate.

"I have the whole afternoon," he explains. "The movie I'm in is shooting on location near here but I don't have any scenes until later tonight."

"What's it called?" I stall for time, seriously considering his offer.

"*Death After Dark.* I play the deputy."

I look around the shed, which trapped heat has turned into an oven, and wonder what is keeping me from refrigerated bliss and possible wild sex with a handsome stranger. "I *am* actually working here," I remind him. "This isn't my stand. I run it for someone else."

"'Okay." He glances at the display of wilted produce and back at me. "How much to buy everything?" He reaches in his hip pocket and produces a wallet. "I don't suppose you take plastic."

I'm taken aback. I can't imagine these limp vegetables and squishy fruit being worth more than a couple hundred tops. Before I can say anything, he hands me five hundred dollars, counting crisp twenties and fifties into my palm.

"Now can you take a break?" he asks.

I don't know if accepting the money turns me into a hooker but I put the cash in the register drawer and turn to him. "Let me help you carry your groceries to the car."

"That's all right. I only want a few pieces of fruit. You can keep the rest." He's flashing me a deep pair of dimples and shiny white teeth.

I imagine those teeth nibbling on my nipples. They instantly peak even harder against my shirt.

We bag up peaches, cantaloupe, raspberries and blackberries, and lock up the stand, then I'm sliding into the buttery leather seats of his car. Cold air blasts my face and rap blasts my eardrums. He turns down the music and asks me questions about myself.

I tell him I'm on summer break and that I'm studying toward an English degree for some foolish reason.

He says he didn't go to college and although he likes acting, sometimes he regrets not having gotten a degree.

By the time we've exchanged all this we're at his hotel. It's not too fancy. I'm surprised, but I figure this movie he's in must be a made-for-TV type with a limited budget.

We enter the room. Now that we're here, I'm more than a little nervous. I've occasionally gone home from keggers with guys I barely know and slept with them, but this feels different. Maybe because I'm not drunk.

The air-conditioning dries my sweat and my skin feels stiff. I really want to freshen up with a shower. Tom has other ideas. He sets down the bag of produce and moves in close to me.

I feel overpowered by his maleness and wilt against him. My hands press against his chest and it's hard. I tilt my face up to accept his kiss and smell the spicy, woodsy aroma of his cologne—not too strong, just right.

Closing my eyes, I revel in the pressure of his lips covering mine. He's a good kisser. He's probably had lots of practice with actresses on his show. Our mouths move together greedily. I can still taste a hint of peach on his soft, wet tongue. His arms around me are strong. His hands slide up and down my back in a comforting caress.

I relax into this, stroking my fingers up his neck and into his softly curling hair. Even though I don't watch "Wild Hearts," I have to admit that it's kind of a thrill to be making out with a real, live TV star.

After a few moments he looks down at me through heavy-lidded eyes and says, "Time for that picnic." His hands move on my shoulder, pushing the straps of my tank top down. I wear no bra underneath. It's one of those shirts with the built-in cups so it is easy for him to uncover my breasts. They pop out of the front of the shirt, full and ripe, the nipples erect and red as rasp-berries. He leans down to suck one into his mouth.

I gasp at the heat and wetness and the pulling sensation that extends all the way down to my crotch.

"Mm, nice," he says when at last he pulls away. "But they need something." He goes to the paper bag and pulls out a peach. Coming back to me, he squeezes the fruit and the skin breaks letting juice trickle down my chest and over each breast. Before it can drip from my nipples onto my shirt, he leans in and sucks it up. The feeling of his tongue bathing my breasts and the sight of his mouth moving all over me; his thick, dark eyelashes closed in rapture; makes me incredibly horny. I imagine how it must taste, the fructose mixed with the salt from my skin.

Tom evidently loves it and keeps licking and sucking long after the juice is gone.

Quickly now, he strips me. My shirt flies one way, my shorts and panties another. I kick off my sandals and tug on Tom's shirt.

Underneath it, his chest, arms and abs are as sculpted as a male model's. I bet he has a personal trainer and works out for hours every day. Must be hell to have your face and body be your fortune and to have to work to maintain them. He's so beautiful I feel a little embarrassed about my less-than-toned body—but only a little. Self-consciousness has never troubled me much.

Besides, Tom's eyes tell me that I look pretty good to him. He asks me to lie on the bed, then he searches around the room for something.

"What?" I ask.

"A knife." Realizing how that might sound he adds, "To cut the fruit."

"I take it you were never a Boy Scout," I tease, shifting on the bed and splaying my legs a little to entice him.

He looks at me blankly with those chocolate-drop eyes and I have to explain, "Not prepared. No pocket knife. Why don't you call the front desk?"

There are perks in being a pseudo-celebrity. Whoever is working the desk hops to it when they get Tom's call. A paring knife is delivered to the door in the time it takes me to unzip Tom's jeans and start sucking him off. His cock is thick and pulsing and he has a hard time tucking it back in his fly when he goes to answer the door.

"Here, Mr. Stander," says a gushing, breathless female voice. "If there's anything else I can get for you…"

I suppress a giggle, imagining her eyes bugging out at seeing him shirtless.

"Thanks. This is all I need." The door is closed and he's back beside me on the bed in seconds. I watch as he cuts into the melon, slicing a thick wedge, scooping the seeds into the wastebasket then cubing it. He lays the melon slices in a neat line down my body from chest to groin. They're slippery. The juice trickles down my rib cage and tickles. It drips onto the bed on either side of me. I believe we're going to totally trash the bedcover before we're through.

Tom's tongue pokes out, resting against his upper lip as he concentrates. It's endearing. Coupled with that floppy dark lock of hair on his forehead, it makes him look like a boy. He cuts into a peach, making thin wedges and arranging them artistically alongside the melon. I watch my naked torso turn into a fruit plate as he scatters handfuls of bright red and dark blackberries across the landscape of my body.

My contours are not flat and the berries start to tumble off of me, but Tom picks them up and mashes them into place. As he approaches my groin, I tilt my head up from the pillow to see what he will do. He squeezes the berries in his hand and lets the juice ooze through his fingers. The rich red and purple juice drips on my pubic mound, slithers on my inner thighs and sweetens my labia. It's the most erotic thing I've ever seen.

Tom rises, wipes his hand off on his jeans, then takes them off. He stands naked by the bed looking at picnic-me for a few moments.

I twitch a little under his gaze, eager for him to start feasting on me. My eyes are drawn to his sharp hip bones, tapered waist, jutting cock. I'm thinking that when he's done with me I'll dribble nectar all over his dick and suck it off.

Finally he moves. He sinks onto the bed next to me and leans down to delicately pick up a chunk of melon from my breastbone with his teeth. He chews and swallows then licks the puddle of juice from my chest. My heart pounds under his tongue and my chest heaves. The smell of ripe fruit is as thick in the air as if we were lying in a garden.

He moves down to my breasts where he has smeared handfuls of berry pulp. He laps the purple and red mounds until there is only a slight lavender stain left behind. My breathing grows shallower as he sucks and nibbles my tits. My nipples ache with desire and so does my crotch.

Tom moves down between my breasts, eating bites of peach and melon from my quivering stomach. The touch of his mouth on my flesh is sending waves of lust throughout my body. The effort of holding still, maintaining a flat surface, is getting more difficult. I want to squirm and writhe under that softly moving mouth.

By the time he reaches my crotch, I'm ready to scream. The sticky, slippery sensation of juice coating my body makes me feel like some pagan offering. My eyes drift closed as his nibbling, licking mouth finally delves between my thighs. I part my legs farther to encourage him and he laps over my pussy, devouring the berries he has mashed there.

When he parts the folds to explore inside, I'm so excited that I almost come the moment his tongue finally reaches and bathes my clit. My hips arch off the bed and I moan. He moans too, loving my body's eager response to his touch.

The gentle, insistent stroking of his tongue stirs me deep inside. There is a mounting pressure, a hard knot that swells and swells like ripening fruit until it bursts into rich, juicy plumpness. I am wet and slippery inside and out and gasping for air like a swimmer surfacing.

"More," I beg. "Just a little more. I'm almost there."

He gives it to me, swirling his tongue around my clit like he's sucking up the last drops of berry syrup from his morning pancakes.

Sunlight explodes behind my closed eyelids. The cosmos flashes past and the rich abundance of earth fills my senses. I hear myself crying out and it sounds far away. I am someplace...other.

When I come down from my high, breathing hard, sweat

cooling in the chill air, Tom is already crawling up my body. He pauses here and there on the way to eat a missed piece of peach or morsel of melon. Finally he faces me, supported above me on those phenomenal biceps. "You taste so good," he murmurs.

I melt. "Your tongue is amazing," I reply.

Wrapping my arms around his back, I pull him against my sticky body. I feel his rigid cock pressing against my cunt. Despite all he's eaten, Tom's eyes still have a hungry look. I suggest a condom and he quickly takes care of that detail, then he's right back between my legs begging admittance. I tilt my hips up and welcome him inside.

He groans as he thrusts deep. I love a noisy lover and Tom is full of words. "You're so hot. Your pussy's so wet." He gives a commentary of his experience as he fills me again and again. His words spill over me and spur me to a new level of lust. It's satisfying to be told you're sexy and beautiful and that he's "never felt anything like this before," even if you have your doubts about the last one. The novelty of the picnic on my body coupled with the extreme hotness of the man plunging into me has me fully aroused. I feel the swirling forces of orgasm gathering once again.

As our skin slaps together, belly to belly, groin to groin, we stick a little. I'm a sugar-coated treat. I scratch my nails down his back and wrap my legs around his hips, pulling him in even deeper.

He pants and blows into my neck as he thrusts faster. His words are gone now, replaced by animal grunting that is just as sexy.

I clench my inner muscles tight around his stabbing shaft, intent on feeling him inside my body. I am so wet that he slides slickly in and out. It reminds me of the sensation of the peach juice trickling down my skin.

My excitement mounts when his speed and guttural groans increase. Finally he cries out and bites my shoulder as he comes.

I scream at the pain and come, hard.

Our bodies keep thrusting toward each other from momentum, slowly decelerating into a gentle pulsing. We're both breathing hard and sweating like the room is ninety degrees instead of a cool seventy-two.

He collapses on top of me, letting me bear his weight. It is welcome and warm.

I turn my head to kiss the soft, dark hair that brushes my cheek. Part of me is in shock, watching all of this like an impartial observer. The gorgeous man, the crazy sex; this was certainly not how I expected my day to turn out.

After a bit we get up and shower together, taking our time soaping away the stickiness on every inch of each other's bodies. By the time we emerge from the bathroom, steam has clouded the motel room as well. We lie on the bed wrapped in towels. Tom orders pizza and we eat it while we watch "Green Acres" on TV Land.

Then I get us both sticky again when I cut open another peach and suck the juice off Tom's cock. The room smells like a summer orchard.

Much later he drops me off at the stand and thanks me for the amazing day. He's a gentleman and waits while I cash out the register, put the money in the bank pouch, then get my car started.

I wave.

He waves.

We drive off in opposite directions.

The rest of the summer I find myself watching "Wild Hearts" despite the fact that it's a crappy show. I'm sucked in. I have to find out if Bobby ends up with adorable Mara or that hateful, backstabbing, two-faced Angelique. When Tom Stander takes his shirt off for a lovemaking scene, I remember how his skin felt under my hands.

Fall begins and so do my classes. But one crisp, cool fall Saturday I'm working at the farm market, sorting Jonathan apples by size into peck bags. This is the time of year I enjoy working here. The scent of apples is sharp and tangy and mixes with the warm, yeasty aroma of fresh-made doughnuts. Squash, gourds and pumpkins lie in colorful piles and jugs of apple cider are available for sale in the cooler.

A car pulls up in front of the stand. I'm adding red and green apples to the top of a bag and don't really pay attention. The car door slams and a moment later someone clears his throat behind me.

"Are those ripe yet?"

I grin and turn slowly around, balancing an apple on my palm. "Apples aren't like summer fruit. You don't pick them until they're completely ripe or they'll be sour. Have a taste."

Tom accepts the fruit from my hand and crunches into it. "Mm, tart."

"Apples also don't make the juice you get with peaches and melons," I warn him. "But we sell apple cider, which is very sticky, and we have hot, soft, squishy, sweet doughnuts." I emphasize every adjective.

He laughs and almost chokes on his apple. "Sounds delicious."

"What are you doing here?" I ask.

"Reshoots." He glances around. "Of course all the leaves are a different color now so I don't know how that's supposed to work." He shakes his head then adds, "I hoped you'd still be here."

"Appearing every weekend through fall."

"Are you almost done working today?"

I glance at my watch. "I've got another four hours."

"Hm." He expresses disappointment, blowing out an annoyed breath. "Well...how much will it cost me to buy everything in the stand?"

I laugh as I turn the sign in front of the stand from OPEN to CLOSED.

SIXTH SENSE

Teresa Noelle Roberts

A psychic advisor?" I shook my head. "Why doesn't he just call himself a con man and have done with it?"

"You must think my mother's an idiot." My client smiled the utter minimum necessary to get the point across, as if to diminish the risk of wrinkles. "And she is pretty naïve. She's always been sheltered, first by her parents, then by Dad. She lives in a prettier world than the one the rest of us see, and the lawyers and the accountant keep her from doing anything too dumb." She gave a graceful shrug. Even in distress, Melissa Demos was graceful. She seemed the kind of woman who had spent so much time honing her beautiful gestures that she could keep them up now without thinking about it. "Spending thousands of dollars on the rose garden or making grants to starving artists who between you and me deserve to be starving—that's eccentric, but harmless. Charming, even. But I'm not going to let her marry a so-called psychic advisor half her age who's obviously in it for the money."

Takes one to know one. Melissa Demos stood to inherit a considerable fortune when her mother died, but what she had now was good looks and a modest trust fund—modest compared to the luxury in which she'd been raised, at least. I'd done a bit of research when she called to make the appointment, since I usually don't get clients from her elegant neighborhood. The number of pictures of her at society parties on the arms of various wealthy executives led me to conclude that her career goal was "trophy wife." I was surprised she was still on the market. She was knock-your-clothes-off gorgeous: wavy dark hair, huge green eyes and the best body youth, good genes and money could combine to produce. Maybe blondes were more fashionable? Or maybe I wasn't the only one who found something a little off-putting about her? I couldn't put a finger on what bothered me. It was possible I was just being catty about someone who had the effrontery to be ten years my junior, beautiful and an heiress.

She interrupted my musings. "So, can you do this?"

"Find out if, as we suspect, Max Shaw is a fraud who makes a habit of getting between lonely older ladies and their money? If it's true, I can get the evidence."

After the contractual details were complete and I pocketed my retainer check, I offered my hand. She shook it perhaps a little too fervently. "Thank you, Carla," she said, equally fervently. "You're a lifesaver."

Maybe that was why she made me uncomfortable, I thought. She was just this side of too much, from her perfect makeup to the handshake. The surface was charming, but seemed a bit contrived to me.

Surface charm was also not lacking in Melissa's potential stepfather. I studied the picture she'd left me. For some reason I'd expected the psychic advisor to be exotic-looking and effete. Instead, he was fair-haired and handsome in a rugged, outdoorsy way that appealed to me, with broad shoulders, tight hips and a killer smile that, in this picture at least, appeared sincere. Then again, he was standing in the middle of the Taj Mahal of rose gardens and probably smiling at the thought of how much money he could get from the Demos vaults before Mama Demos realized she was being duped.

He looked tall, although it was hard to tell, since he was alone in the picture and I wasn't sure how tall five-hundred-dollar rose bushes are. And young enough that I could see why Melissa Demos was concerned—older than she was, but certainly younger than her mom. Around my age, in fact.

I was going to be keeping tabs on this man. Poking into various facets of his life. Trying to prove he was malicious and sleazy at best and criminal at worst.

Give me an ugly suspect anytime. I don't like investigating someone I'd rather be dating. You find out the bad things about a guy soon enough—I'd rather have some fun with him before getting disillusioned.

I tracked down a few things following paper and online trails. Max Shaw seemed to be his real name and he actually was a psychic advisor. By that, I mean he had been calling himself one for several years before he met Mrs. Demos, and had a website and a business that advertised in some of the New Age rags. He'd even been on a couple of local talk shows, doing the whole "I can read your deepest wishes" routine. It seemed as legitimate as something so flaky could be. There are outright con artists, and then there are those who really believe what they're doing, and on the surface he seemed the latter.

A little more research led me to some of his clients. So far, nothing backed up Melissa's fears. I didn't come across any-one who'd had her life savings sucked away—or who even had enough life savings to be worth the effort. None of them even hinted that he'd taken money from them, except relatively mod-est fees for readings, but some of them got flustered at the sound of his name. Curiously, or maybe not, they were always the good-looking ones, not the little old ladies, who just said what a charming young man he was, and how good his readings were.

It was Rose Perez who provided the missing link. "Client? That was how I met him: going to the psychic reader on a girls' night out. But what I really am to him is an ex-lover. Or maybe I should say ex-slave."

She stared at me with hard dark eyes, challenging me to judge her.

Rose was the business brains behind a successful Caribbean-fusion restaurant. On the wall behind her, I could see her framed Wharton MBA. Even at this brief meeting, the words that came to mind to describe her were *smart* and *tough*. "You don't seem the type," I said cautiously. I'd learned what little I knew of the whole S&M thing from reading trashy novels. I'd bet most of it was as wrong as what you learn about private detectives from mysteries.

"I never knew I was until I met Max," Rose said. "He saw a side of me that I never even knew was there." Her expression soft-ened. "We didn't last—it was all about the sex—but I'll always be grateful to him. If it hadn't been for him, I never would have... Well, let's just say my life would be a lot duller." For the first time I wondered about the delicate choker she was wearing. A collar? I'd always envisioned something made of leather and steel, but I guess you couldn't wear that with a smart business suit.

Rose didn't add any other bombshells to the Max Shaw story. She hadn't spent any money on him, other than the cost of the initial reading and a few special dinners out, and he'd never asked for it. He seemed sincere about the psychic business, and good at it, but it didn't seem like they'd talked much about it.

I left the office shaking my head. Who knew that someone like Rose would like being on the receiving end of the whips and chains and serve-me-you-slut thing? *Well, whatever makes you happy*, I told myself.

It certainly made me more curious to meet Max Shaw. If he could seduce someone as smart as Rose Perez, I could see how he'd be able to charm the pants—literally—off a lonely, naïve older woman with more money than sense.

When I found myself checking out S&M websites that night, I told myself it was research. At first it was, but I have to admit my curiosity grew to be more than professional. There were plenty of lurid images, but from some of the more factual sites I could see it wasn't about abuse, except in edgy fantasies; it was more about strong sensation and control.

Strong sensation I could appreciate. I'd always enjoyed the kind of rough-and-tumble sex where scratches, bite marks and accidental bruises were part of the game, and it wasn't a stretch to see that spanking and slapping might be fun. Maybe even whipping, although that conjured up some scary *Mutiny on the Bounty* images. I wasn't about to give up control to any man, though.

But the more I read, the more I thought about it, the more *taking* control sounded hot.

And the more I thought about it—the more my musings turned into full-blown fantasies—the more I found myself picturing a man falling prey to my not-so-tender mercies. A man who looked a lot like Max Shaw, to be specific. I've always had a thing for the tall, fair, outdoorsy type, and it added a fillip to the fantasy to think about inflicting my will on a man who could turn a bright woman like Rose Perez into his slave.

Max made it ridiculously easy to talk with him. Leaching off Mrs. Demos or not, he still had a psychic reading business in one of the artsy neighborhoods near the university, so I set up an appointment with him.

I wasn't sure what to expect from a psychic's office—would it be like a gypsy fortune-teller's den in a movie or more like a doctor's office? As it turned out, it looked like a home office decorated by someone with New Age leanings: a desk covered with paper, some worn but comfortable-looking chairs, a lot of funky decorations with a vaguely ethnic flavor, a poster of Glastonbury Tor. There wasn't a receptionist or anything; apparently he just trusted that people would show up at the right time for their appointments.

I didn't even manage to take a seat before I blew it. I'd not spoken more than a few sentences before Max shook his head at me in disgust. "You're not even doing a good job of pretending to be interested in my services, Carla. You're asking the wrong questions. And you can't hide your skepticism." His voice was rich and seductive even with the hint of anger in it. He had stood up and moved around the desk while we were talking and now he was uncomfortably close to me, close enough that I could smell his cologne—something that hinted of leather and green herbs, light but noticeable.

"Okay, you caught me. I'm pretty skeptical about the whole thing, but I'm curious too." I tried to look nonchalant. Usually I was good at the looking-nonchalant bit, but I didn't think he was buying it. "One of my friends told me you'd given her some amazing insights. Maybe you remember her—Rose Perez."

"I remember her," he said calmly. "I'm glad she found our

sessions valuable." I looked for any one of the telltale signs I'd expect from someone who'd just had an ex-slave's name dropped during what was supposed to be a business discussion. He didn't show any of them. The guy was good.

"So I was wondering if…"

Max moved even closer. This time I backed up. He was a lot bigger than I was, but that wasn't the point. He was exuding a different flavor of menace, all pheromones and contained power. "You were wondering," he drawled. "I'm sure you were. Isn't that what private detectives are paid to do, to wonder and ponder and ask questions?" I wanted to ask him how he knew, but I didn't have a chance. "But I think more than your job led you here, if you've talked to Rose."

His hands closed on my shoulders and he pulled me close. I felt a second of exhilaration, some kind of primal response to being held so possessively by such a handsome man. In that second, I could understand Rose—and maybe Mrs. Demos.

A second was about as long as I wanted to feel like a quivering mass of submissive femininity. Then I performed a tidy little judo move that got Max down on his back with me standing over him.

All my fantasies came back to haunt me.

As sexy as he was on his feet and taking control of the conversation, he looked even sexier in the position he was now in. The look of confusion on his formerly assured face was priceless as it dawned on him. "You're partly right. You've been on my mind ever since I had that enlightening conversation with Ms. Perez. But I'm no submissive."

Then I considered my options.

The smart one would be to walk away from the situation. Leave before I did something stupid enough to ruin my career and possibly my whole life. Give Melissa Demos back the retainer, come up with some excuse to mask the fact that I had a bad case of kinky lust for the person I was supposed to be investigating.

Instead I reached down, took his tie off, and ripped his shirt open. You know, they just don't sew buttons on the way they used to. Max's eyes widened, but to my surprise, he didn't say a word, or even try to move from the position he'd ended up in.

I'd like to think that if he'd protested, even a little, I'd have stopped.

I'd like to think so, but I can't be sure, because as soon as I touched him, the blood all rushed from my brain to my crotch and I started seeing everything through the black-and-blue lens of my own desire. I'd never wanted anything as badly as I wanted Max Shaw tied up and ready for my use.

His pants and underwear were a little harder to deal with, but when I barked, "Lift your hips, bitch," he complied word-lessly.

He looked even better naked. I do appreciate a man who makes the effort to keep in shape.

When I pulled the belt free from his belt loops, he whimpered like a scared puppy, a surprisingly small noise from such a big man. At the same time, though, his cock stirred for the first time. Up until now he'd been compliant, but only as if he were too confused to react otherwise. This was different.

I considered using the belt as he obviously expected me to but decided to put that off until I had him secured. Better safe than sorry—the evidence of his cock said he was getting into it, but he was big and despite my judo training, small and skillful wouldn't necessarily overcome big and angry. I used the belt to bind his feet together. He put up a perfunctory fight, but I threw my weight across him and kept him still. I'd have preferred a classic spread eagle, but the office just wasn't configured for it.

His silk tie went to tie his arms across his broad chest, wrist to forearm.

As a finishing touch I shoved his underwear into his mouth, making the gesture as dramatic as possible while taking care not to choke him. The green briefs drooped out either side, making him look like a retriever puppy who'd been practicing "retrieving" from the laundry pile. He rolled his head back and forth a few times, but didn't make a real effort to get rid of them.

"I don't know which is funnier," I said with my best affected sneer, "the psychic who didn't see this coming or the top who's getting a hard-on from being tied up and humiliated. You're loving this, aren't you?"

He nodded tightly, just once. There was a feverish glow to his face—fear and desire and amazement—that made him look even more handsome. His fat cock was getting harder by the second.

No doubt about it, I was loving this too. I'd gone from merely slick to drenched right through my jeans. Looking at this hot, muscular man trussed up for my delectation, it was all I could do not to strip down, straddle that nice big dick and fuck myself senseless.

Tempting, but in the end too easy. I might never have an opportunity like this again. There was a decent chance I'd end up facing a whole slew of charges for this adventure—I might as well be hanged for a sheep as a lamb.

Max's office wasn't the well-equipped dungeon of fantasy, but I'm imaginative. A quick rummage through his desk drawers yielded a wooden ruler, a spare phone cord, rubber bands and a handful of really nasty binder clips. And a few clothespins. I couldn't figure out what they were doing in his desk until I remembered some of the things I'd seen on line the night before and grinned. Apparently the man liked to be prepared. He probably had some other toys stashed somewhere, but I wasn't feeling patient enough to look. My own possessions weren't too useful but I did have a claw-style hair clip in my bag that had some potential. And of course, I had my own belt.

"The question, of course," I said out loud, walking around his bound form, "is where to start. What would you do in my position, if you had a woman tied up like this? Would you kick her a few times, just to show her who's boss?" I nudged his hip with the toe of my boot as I said it, hardly a kick, but enough to make my point. "Or torture her nipples a little?" I swooped down, knelt next to him, and put clothespins on his nipples. "Or cause a little pain elsewhere?" I put binder clips on his inner thighs, one on each side near the groin. He winced so prettily that I added two more. Those were going to leave marks. Nice.

I surveyed my handiwork so far. "You might do something like that. But then I bet you'd beat her." That was when I got out the ruler.

I started with light blows on the pecs, concentrating on the area close to his nipples. I'd never done anything like this before but it felt right, like I was born to watch red streaks form on a man's skin, born to watch him squirm as best he could while tied up, born to rake the nails of my free hand across his chest hard enough that welts rose behind them.

Born to watch his hips twitch up and down, helpless in his lust.

"Which is better?" I asked. "This"—a slap with the ruler— "or this?"—a gouge with my nails. He tried to answer. Since he couldn't really do it around the underwear in his mouth, I repeated the question, and the demonstration, several times. Finally I decided that he was saying they were both good. It seemed that way from his reactions, anyway.

His chest was nice and rosy now, so I moved on. A flurry of smacks on his well-toned belly made him jump. Then I traveled to his thighs, where I figured I could step up the intensity.

Two good wallops and Max made a noise that I could distinguish through the underwear gag as "Oh, yeah." I'd have found it hard to believe—I certainly wouldn't have liked being hit that hard—except that a pearl of pre-come was glistening on the head of his cock.

"Now, dear," I said, "we can't have you enjoying yourself too much. I'm not done with you yet." I placed the open hair clip around his cock and then ever so slowly closed it. I didn't figure it would be all that painful, but I had to imagine it was nerve-wracking, especially with me closing it so slowly. He was clenching his teeth around the underwear, lines of strain on his face, but his hard-on didn't falter.

Again I surveyed my handiwork. Max was a sight all right—red-faced, tied up with his own accessories, damp briefs in his mouth, ordinary household objects decorating his flesh and a purple plastic hair clip on his dick. It should have been ridiculous, but it was the hottest thing I'd ever seen. The marks I'd left on his skin only made it better.

"Where was I?" I murmured, falsely absentminded as I brought the ruler down with a resounding crack across his thighs. Then I had an idea. I remembered reading that you had to take tight clips off after a while. What if I *thwacked* one off?

I heard the yelp through the gag.

The yelp and the throaty growl that immediately followed it. Pain and pleasure, perfectly balanced.

The power of it reverberated right through me, making my insides quiver as it passed to my clit. His eyes had gone very dark and seemingly far away but I knew he was in the moment about as intensely as it's possible to be. I knew it because I was too, and right now we were connected as I'd rarely been connected to another man, even ones I'd loved.

Psychic? Maybe there was something to it. At least I knew damn well what he wanted right now, and it was what I wanted too.

Another carefully aimed smack popped off the other binder clip. They left behind angry welts where they'd pinched his skin. I hit him a few more times for good measure. Then I repeated the procedure with the clothespins on his nipples.

"What now?" I mused out loud.

He muttered something into the gag. Suddenly I was tired of that joke and pulled the underpants out of his mouth. "What was that?"

"Let me eat you," he begged, his eyes bright and appealing. I'd never heard a guy so eager to lick my cunt before, and I've been lucky enough to have some lovers who really liked it.

Very tempting. But there was something I wanted to do first. "Patience," I said, not sure if I were talking more to him or to myself. "Your chance will come, Max. And your chance to come will come. Just not yet."

I took the clip off his dick. His sigh of relief changed to something quite different when I replaced it with a few loops of phone cord. I'm not sure how to describe the noise but both *yes* and *no* were involved, with *yes* winning out.

"Roll over," I commanded, and was thrilled by how quickly he obeyed. It couldn't have been the most comfortable position to lie in, especially with parts of him rather tender, but he didn't flinch.

He did flinch when I doubled my belt over and brought it down hard on his ass. Then he said, "Thank you," in a voice that was choked with pain and lust.

I liked that simple "thank you." I liked it almost as much as the powerful thrill of leather snapping against skin. How could I have reached my midthirties and not known how right it felt to get thanked for turning a man's ass red?

Hmm, it wasn't red yet, just sporting one nice pink mark. I'd have to work on that.

Twenty blows later—I had him count—his ass was red all right. In fact, some parts were purple and welted and looked like they'd stay bruised for a while. But that wasn't why I stopped. I needed some release, needed it to the point that it hurt. And unlike Max, I don't like to suffer.

I had him roll back over—I could almost feel him wince as his butt came into contact with the rough carpet—and shucked my clothes. "Now, Max," I purred, "you've been a very good boy. Here's your reward." I straddled his face, then leaned forward for balance as I ground my dripping crotch against his mouth.

I can't honestly say whether Max was gifted with great oral talent or just a lot of enthusiasm. At that point, I was so wrought up that a few licks were all it took to reduce me to screaming, twitching ecstasy.

I kept him going for more than a few licks, though. When you have a captive cunnilingist, you might as well take advantage of it, right?

When I'd finally had enough, I slithered off him and collapsed on the floor next to him, too spent to move at first. Then I realized there were a few things I had to do before I let myself pass out.

First the phone cord came off his engorged, purple cock. Then I untied his arms. "I promised you a chance to come, Max. Now play with yourself for me." There was a second's hesitation—I don't know if it was shyness even after all I'd done to him or just trouble convincing his hands to move. Then he obeyed.

"Don't hold back," I urged. "I want to see your come squirting all over the place. Do it. Come for me."

He didn't need much encouragement. Like me, he'd been holding back for a long time.

It was the first time ever that the sound and sight of a man coming triggered a mini-orgasm in me.

For a while we lay there side by side on the coarse rug. I was too drained to think about why I was in Max Shaw's office at all, and I suspect he was further gone than I was. I think I dozed off for a while, then woke with a start to find him undoing the belt around his ankles.

Everything refocused into painful clarity—the Demos case, my impulsive actions, all the very good reasons Max might want revenge. No matter how much fun it had ended up being, it still had started out more like rape. I started scrambling away.

"Relax," he said. "I'm not angry. Far from it. I knew what you wanted and needed from me, and I was more than happy to give it."

I snorted. "Psychic powers. Right."

"No." His voice was very serious, serious enough that it compelled me to listen. "Not in the way people usually mean it. I do think there's a sixth sense—call it intuition. Practically everyone has it, but in some of us it's more developed. It makes a good psychologist, a good detective—you'd know about that. Or a good psychic. I can figure out a lot about what a person wants and needs from clues she isn't even aware of herself. The rest might be guesswork or maybe there's really something more to it, but I'm right more often than not. It's not magic. And it's not a con. People want guidance and advice. I provide it. And I try to make it useful to them."

"How did you know...?"

"That you were a detective? That's easy. Google. Same way you knew how to find my office."

"That's cheating."

"That's *research*."

"You're supposed to be a psychic! Anyway, I meant how did you know about...?" I was suddenly tongue-tied, a far cry from the confident dominatrix I'd been a little while before.

Max laughed. "Practice and intuition and in the end a lucky guess. A person in the scene learns to look for certain clues that someone else might be of like mind. I just seem to be better at it than most."

We laughed. And then we both fell silent, aware of the weight that still lay between us.

He brought it up first. "Did Melissa Demos hire you?"

I nodded. Somehow after what we'd just done, I couldn't treat him like a suspect.

"It figures. I had it coming." He sighed, hesitated, then continued. "Melissa and I were lovers. Normally I'm a top, but as you've seen, some women bring out the other side in me and Melissa was one of them. She played me like a guitar, and I fell in love with her. And that's what got me into trouble."

I nodded. It might all be a lie, but I could see Melissa being toppy, and then using it to manipulate people. It would be nice to think I hadn't just disliked her because she was beautiful, but because I knew instinctively that she was a bitch.

Now I had another reason to dislike her. I'd really enjoyed feeling like I was the first to make Max want to submit.

"Melissa said she'd be my Mistress full-time if I could help her siphon enough money away from her mom that she could live in the proper style. And like a fool I said yes." His face was a mottled red, and he looked away from me as he continued. "I'm not a bad person. You've seen what I charge for readings. This isn't a get-rich-quick scam—it's a way to make my own hours and sometimes meet women. But for a while there, I wanted to live with Melissa, to serve her, to obey her in every way, even with something as shady as that. You have no idea what stupid

things will go through your head when you're in love with a
twisted top."

"So why did she hire me?"

"Because I actually got to know her mom. Kate Demos is a
wonderful woman, far more intelligent and creative than anyone has ever given her credit for. She married very young and
her husband liked having this cute little innocent wife. She's finally coming into her own as a widow, but she's still unsure of
herself, and it would have been really easy for me as the 'psychic
advisor' to rip her off and then hurt her terribly. I couldn't do
that—and when I realized Melissa *could*, to her own mother,
the lust-blinders came off. I broke up with her. She must want
revenge—and probably to get me away from her mother before
I let Kate know what an evil bitch her daughter really is."

"Melissa said you were going to marry her mom."

"Well, I did say I'd rather marry Kate than her any day.
And she may really believe I'm after her mom's money. Melissa's greedy herself, so I think she'd have a hard time believing I
wouldn't take that opportunity if I had it." He smiled. "I can't
honestly say I'd mind marrying an attractive, wealthy older
woman, but there's nothing like that between us. Between you
and me, one of the things she wanted to talk with a psychic
about is that she's fallen for this wonderful lesbian and wanted
to know if she should pursue the romance."

"And you said?"

"I said it's always scary exploring a new facet of yourself,
but you miss out on a lot if you don't." He reached out, took
my hands. "And Carla, I'd say the same thing to you. That's
not some psychic thing, that's just advice from someone who's
been there."

I left Max Shaw's office with almost as many questions as I came in with, but they were different questions. With my whole body buzzing with hormones, I would have liked to swallow Max's story, but my instinct—what he called my sixth sense—suggested that what he'd told me was an oversimplification at best. If Melissa had known I'd find nothing particularly incriminating, she had nothing to gain by hiring me except the petty pleasure of annoying Max. Either she was just too suspicious for her own good, as Max implied, or Max was lying through his teeth about something.

I'd have to investigate a little further, I decided. And the investigation would involve some very stringent interrogation of Max Shaw.

TIED TO THE KITCHEN SINK

Kay Jaybee

Hi, you must be Will; happy birthday." The girl smiled a dazzlingly white set of teeth in his direction, as she turned her head away from the washing up.

Will stopped dead. He had gone through Ben's back door into the kitchen expecting it to be deserted as usual, but it wasn't.

It wasn't her smile that caused Will's feet to feel as if they'd become super-glued to the floor, and his trousers to tighten. It was the fact that she stood there in long, black high-heeled boots and absolutely nothing else.

"You look a little pale," the girl said, eyes twinkling, "why don't you have a little sit-down over there." She pointed to an armchair in the corner of the room. "I can't join you, I'm afraid." She raised her hands, revealing long, thin, silver chains attaching her to the faucet taps. "I'm tied to the kitchen sink at the moment." As she laughed, the dark pigtails that hung down her back bobbed against her bare flesh.

"Um, well, I..." Will stumbled over his words as his eyes

scanned every inch of her. "Where's...?"

"Ben?" she finished for him. "At the pub. He thought you would enjoy your birthday present more if he wasn't here. I'm Karen."

"Karen?"

"Are you okay? Ben seemed to think that I was exactly what you wanted for your twenty-first. If not, perhaps you could unlock me." She indicated a small pile of keys on the table, conveniently placed next to a pack of condoms. "Ben said that you had fantasized about finding a woman tied to the sink." She looked up through her fringe with mock shyness.

Will was torn between thoughts of simply walking out, or untying the girl, or...who was he kidding? His head swam with erotic images. She was real. He'd already pinched himself and this was not a dream. His dick stirred as he stared at her.

She was tall and slim, and her tanned skin shone against the dull kitchen units. Will focused on the soft flesh that emerged from the top of her killer boots. He could almost taste her already.

"Who are you?" Will took a deep breath and walked toward the sink. *Why the hell not?* he thought. *A gift is a gift....*

"I told you, I'm Karen." She sighed as he trailed a finger around her neck. His hard, denim-encased cock rubbed against her arse as he stood close behind her. "A friend of Ben's. You thought I was a hooker?"

"Well I..."

"You aren't the only one with fantasies, you know." She stroked his cheek with her polished silver nails. "I've seen your picture on his mobile." She turned as much as her tethers would allow and ran wet hands over his thin shirt. "Now, I think that's enough questions. What would you like to do for your birthday?"

She looked at him beseechingly. "Are you going to leave me

tied here to do all this awful washing up, Sir? Or are you going to let me have a little lie down on that nice table? Or maybe a rest in that armchair?"

Will smiled; obviously, Ben had explained his friend's fantasy to her. He was in charge. He stripped off his damp shirt and stood next to her in just his jeans. "I think you should stay exactly where you are until all that work is done, don't you?"

"Oh, but Sir, I am in so much need here, and the water is making my skin all dry." Karen looked up at him, playfully batting her eyelashes.

It's like acting out a bad porn movie, Will thought. *Fantastic.* Karen turned her back on him and continued to wash up the dirty dishes that Ben must have ignored for days.

His hands shaking slightly, Will mentally thanked his friend before he reached around the girl; tentatively placing a hand on each firm breast, he let his fingers gently circle them. He smiled as he felt her body shiver. "I think it would be best if you didn't make a sound. Do you understand?" Karen inclined her head, and managed to stifle a cry as Will began to flick his fingers hard against her nipples.

Will stepped back and ran his hands down Karen's smooth back. Dipping his fingers into the top of her boots, he began teasing the skin between them and her rounded arse. Suddenly, he badly wanted her to be less perfect. She was too neat, too willing. Looking around the room Will spotted a tub of cooking utensils. His eye fell on a wooden spoon; he grabbed it and started rubbing it against her flawless buttocks.

Karen shifted back slightly toward the feel the wood. Will could see she ached for more attention; the skin around the top of her legs glistened with the sticky liquid oozing from her pussy. He swung the spoon and hit her hard. If she wanted to get closer to the wood, then so be it.

Karen yelled out, earning herself a second smack. "I told you to be quiet."

"Sorry Sir, you took me by surprise, Sir."

Will admired the crisscross of red marks that the spoon was making on her creamy skin. Each time he connected the wood with her arse she groaned, but to the satisfaction of his straining cock, she didn't move away—in fact she was pushing her arse out further and further, making it an easier target. He gave her one final strike.

Will took several steadying breaths. He would have loved to rip his jeans off and thrust into her there and then, but as much as he wanted to fuck her, he didn't want it to be over, and he didn't think she did either. Anyway, he hadn't completed his fantasy yet.

There was a splash of water and foam as Karen dropped the saucepan she was trying to clean; her legs were shaking. He could see she was as close to the edge as he was. Right now he wanted to see just how close. "Keep working, miss." Karen obediently thrust her hands back into the water, the chains clanking against the contents of the bowl. "Whatever happens, I want you to keep working."

He knelt behind her and cupped a hand between her legs, pushing them open slightly, and felt them quiver against him. When he took his hand away Karen moaned as if feeling the loss. Will no longer cared about her being silent, and he quickly replaced his hand with his tongue, taking one long, leisurely lap at her pussy before kissing her clit over and over again.

The contents of the sink clashed together as Karen dropped whatever she'd been cleaning. Her body bucked against the cupboards as she came against his sucking mouth.

Will tore off his jeans; he couldn't wait much longer. She was willingly making herself his birthday present, and he was damn well going to enjoy every second of this fantasy time with her. Pulling on a condom, he pulled her back toward him and slipped inside her. "Oh god," he groaned into her ear. He felt her tighten around his cock as the last moments of her orgasm ebbed away. "Ready for another one?" he whispered against her ear.

"May I talk, Sir?" Karen asked quietly.

"Oh yes." Will began to move painfully slowly against her, his balls gently swaying as he glided in and out of her soaking snatch.

"Then please, Sir, when you have shot your load inside me, may I be untied? I have something for you."

Will couldn't reply; what the hell could she have for him that might compare to this? He increased his pace, thrusting faster and faster, banging into her with all his might, his hand reaching between her legs. When his fingers found her clit he was rewarded with a scream of satisfaction as Karen thrust herself back against him, frantically trying to keep pace. Finally, Will let go, grunting into her hair, his weight forcing her as far down as her restraints would allow as she shuddered against him.

It took a few seconds before he could move; the force of their fuck had made his head spin. He pulled away, easing Karen back to her feet and resting her against the cupboard whilst he disposed of his condom and grabbed the keys for her chains. He undid the tiny padlocks, and Karen rubbed her wrists. "Happy birthday," she said as she walked away from him. Reaching down underneath the table she pulled out a neatly wrapped present. "I think you should have this now," she said as she perched on the edge of the table.

Will looked into her lust-filled eyes before attacking the wrapping paper. Inside there was a long candle and a small box of matches. He looked at her, confused. She smiled up at him. "It is traditional to have candles on your cake. However, Ben didn't get you a cake, he got you me. I wonder," she said as she lay back onto the table, spreading her legs out in front of him, "if we can find anything around here that could be used as a candleholder?"

THE BUTCH, THE BOY AND ME

Andrea Zanin

He's an interesting kind of guy, my lover. He's small, barely five foot five, and not exactly what you'd call beautiful. But my friend Dag describes him well: "Rob smells like sex," she says. And he does. There's a certain something that just radiates from him, an air of intellectual intensity, a sense of style, the way his frown frames his piercing blue eyes from under his long hair. When he shakes your hand, he touches your skin just a little deeper than most, and when he brushes by you in passing, he leaves invisible trails of inadvertent desire.

Although Rob has never outright mentioned any interest in men, and has quite a fervent appreciation for women, I can't help but think of him as somehow queer. Maybe it's the fact that he's a gender bender, although he might not see himself that way—he actually wears tights when he puts on his kilt and combat boots, and occasionally, the sparkle of a pretty necklace can be seen at his throat. His femininity adds an exciting complexity to his very masculine energy; he's an unusual blend of spices, a paradox, a bi-

nary wrapped up in one person. I like the way he can talk my kind
of politics and he understands that just because I am in his bed a
couple of nights a week doesn't mean he has any claim to my body
or my identity—something that most of the straight boys I've been
with tend to forget after a couple of mind-bending orgasms.

So Dag and I were having dinner the other day. She was looking her usual hot self—there's something about wide shoulders
under a crisp shirt, the perfectly sculpted line of a supershort
haircut at the nape of a smooth neck, soft skin over the strong
lines of a jaw, the hint of wrinkles forming at the corners of an
intelligent mouth, the faint cologne, the perfectly worn jeans.
Dandy butch, she is, and a beautiful one.

Out of the blue she said to me, "You know, I'm almost thirty
years old and I've never slept with a man." She paused, toyed
with her fork. I waited. Where was she going with this? "It's not
that I'm doubting myself as a dyke," she went on, "but sometimes I'd like to know what it's like, you know?"

"Sure," I answered, noncommittal. "A learning experience."

Dag got a wistful look on her face. "But I wouldn't even
know where to start. I never really thought of it before, but all
my friends are women. Hell, even my car mechanic is a chick.
And I can't cruise a guy—what would we do, talk about hockey?
Arm wrestle?"

The waiter came by and asked, "Ma'am, sir, can I get you
anything else?"

"No thanks," she said, not even blinking.

"Dag, not all guys are jocks. Whoever you end up exploring
this with needs to be someone who makes you feel comfortable,
who you feel a connection with."

"What kind of guy would I feel a connection with? That's
just the problem. He'd have to be pretty unusual. You know,
someone like...like..."

"Rob," I said, a warm feeling of anticipation beginning to spread through me.

Saturday night. The dinner was rich, the wine flowed freely, and there was old jazz playing on the stereo. The conversation was full of double entendres and subtle flirtation. There was nothing planned; we were just going to see what would happen.

Dinner was over; we moved to the living room, and brought a bowl of grapes with us. I snuggled into the couch with Rob on my right side and Dag on my left. Dag slipped her arm behind my shoulders; Rob fed me a grape, a burst of sweetness on my tongue. I fed one back, and one to Dag. I put a grape in my mouth, and held another one between two fingers. Something shifted in the air. Rob leaned in to bite the one from between my teeth, and Dag took my fingertips into her mouth, eating the small fruit and running the tip of her tongue over my nails, around the sensitive pads of my fingertips, trailing the edge of her teeth softly over my skin. Her hands rose to hold mine, and she held up each finger in turn, teasing with her teeth. The scent of her shampoo, her clean shirt, her leather boots swirled together with the smell of Rob's skin, his jeans, the hint of cigarette smoke clinging to him, the wine. I breathed deep and tasted them.

There's a particular kind of energy that can be created by three people when they have pleasure in mind. Magic swims through the tension between them, breaking boundaries, softening inhibitions. Rob kissed me full on the mouth, the kind of kiss that makes your heartbeat rise into your eardrums and your body quiver. His kiss pushed me slowly backward; I rested against Dag's shoulder and felt her breath send tingles along my neck. In that moment, the world was reduced to sensations and small sounds, slow movements, skin, hot mouths. Rob kissed me deeper, reaching to support himself with a hand on Dag's thigh. I felt Dag's palms warm on my sides as I reached up to touch Rob's chest, feeling his small, well-formed body under the soft cloth.

The kiss broke off, leaving me breathless. Rob looked up. He and Dag were inches away from one another. I felt a moment of suspense—was she comfortable enough with all this? Rob, ever tuned in to these things, simply waited. I could feel her heart beating fast behind me; I covered her hand with mine and held it, weaving my fingers through hers. She breathed in, reached up and kissed him. She was tentative at first; he followed her lead, their lips just barely touching in exploration. I shifted so that I could watch—my beautiful butch, my sweet boy—two masculinities, worlds apart, figuring out how it might all work between them, tasting one another's difference.

I saw Rob's eyes close, his nostrils flare ever so slightly, as Dag pulled him into the kiss, reaching up to bring him closer, her fingers tightening in his hair. I couldn't turn away; I was riveted. Rob's hand came up from her thigh and moved slowly, exquisitely, from my hip; up my belly, the hot skin of his palm slipping against the thin nylon of my shirt over my breast. He began to tease my nipple through my shirt, his expert fingers stroking gently, sending waves of excitement through me. I made a sound of pleasure and Dag's body responded instinctively; she pushed her hips against me as Rob explored her mouth. I felt the seam of her jeans hot against the small of my back, her belt buckle pressing into my spine. I watched her take Rob's lip between her teeth, worry it, as Rob closed his eyes and let his mouth open slightly. I was so close to them, I could have joined their kiss just by raising my lips, but I let them enjoy it alone for now.

Dag's hand moved up to my breast, and she started in surprise when she touched Rob's hand there, breaking off the kiss with a chuckle. The logistics of threesomes are always fascinating to negotiate. I wriggled out of my warm spot between them and stood as Rob leaned in to nuzzle the side of Dag's neck, the soft skin leading up to her ear. I unbuttoned my shirt partway as she moved to feel his tongue against her neck, and then I straddled Dag's muscular thigh and held my breast to her mouth. She began to suckle it hungrily, and I ground my crotch into her leg as her talented teeth made my pulse race.

Small flowers of blood bloomed under Dag's skin as Rob's mouth worked her throat. I pulled away from her lips and quickly began to undo her shirt. My fingers fumbled in my urgency and Rob took over, gently unhooking each button from its hole. Dag was pinned under the two of us; I ran my fingers through Rob's long hair, pulling against his scalp as he deliberately undid the last button. Modest about her breasts, Dag wore a simple sports bra to keep them out of her way—she'd once told me that her ties lay much better when her chest was minimized under the men's shirts she wore. But despite the incongruity of a man's fingers brushing against her nipples, they were visibly hard through the stretched cotton, and he spread her shirt open to thumb them with both hands. Dag writhed under me, letting out a low groan as I kissed the corners of her mouth and Rob rolled her nipples between his fingertips, ran his nails over them through the stretchy material. The silver of his thumb rings glinted in the low lighting against the square, solid joints of his small hands.

Rob, I realized, had a hard-on straining against his jeans. I moved my attention to him for a moment, sliding down so that I was kneeling on the floor. I ran my finger up the inside of his thigh and he spread his legs; I pressed my knuckles into the bulge at his crotch and rocked my hand back and forth. He raised his hips to meet me, his torso still turned toward Dag and his face now buried in her breasts; he was tonguing one stiff nipple and then the other. With my free hand, I did the same to Dag as I had just done to Rob, and she too spread her legs to let me rub her through her jeans. I got into a rhythm, my hands against the twin spots both pulsing with the heat of their bodies.

Dag cupped her hand under Rob's chin, bringing him up to attack him in breathless, open-mouthed kisses before she pulled his shirt over his head. She gripped a handful of his hair, and brought his throat toward her, biting and kissing from his face down to his collarbone, then down his chest, smooth with just a small patch of fine hair down the hollow of his sternum. She ran her teeth over the fine links of the thin silver chain around his neck, and began to chew his nipples. He let out a ragged moan, and I felt his cock jump under the denim.

Keeping one hand on Rob's cock, I started to unbuckle Dag's jeans with the other as she leaned into Rob, running her short fingernails over the skin of his rib cage while she mercilessly worked at his tender flesh. I quickly realized that their positions would make it almost impossible to get anywhere, so I decided to break the moment.

"Guys," I said. "Let's go to the bedroom and get some clothes off."

Rob's hair was messy and Dag's face flushed. We hurried to the bedroom, where Dag quickly removed her boots and shucked off the remainder of her shirt. I stripped and hopped onto the bed. I sat against the headboard with my legs spread and motioned for Dag to sit with her back to me. She leaned against me and stretched out her legs; Rob kneeled over her, slipping the end of her belt out of its clasp and popping open the buttons of her fly, one by one. She tensed for a moment—second thoughts? No—maybe—but I could see she didn't want to stop. I could smell her cologne in the short hairs on the back of her neck, and as Rob gently pulled her jeans and boxer briefs down her thighs and dropped them on the floor with her belt clanking, I whispered in her ear, "Beautiful boy—my boy, he's going to taste you."

Rob was kissing up the inside of her ankles, up the smoothness of her calves, rubbing into the tender spot behind her knee. He breathed the scent of her, worked his way up her thighs. His long hair spilled over one of her legs as he bent his head to her center, breathing, warming her still more with his hot mouth, almost touching her but not quite. I kissed the side of her face, smoothed my hands over the soft curves of her wide shoulders, cupped her small breasts. Rob's hands pressed her thighs further open, the shiny mother-of-pearl and obsidian of the rings on his middle fingers gleaming against her creamy skin. He dipped his face down, tasting her gently, parting her folds with his tongue. She breathed in sharply through her nose and moved up to meet his mouth, letting him dig deeper into her, feeling him lap at her clit, spreading further to let his tongue probe into the parts that had never been penetrated by anything male.

He closed his eyes and feasted, twisting his tongue against her and teasing her until she made high-pitched noises of wanting, then working one finger into her and stroking that soft place inside while his tongue moved quickly against her clit. Dag's body tensed; she dug her fingers into my calves, into his bent shoulder; she threw her head back, forehead beaded in sweat, and thrust against Rob's diligent mouth and came, sobbing, a red flush spreading over her breasts. Rob laid his head on her thigh and stroked her belly as she rocked, her face contorted.

Rob raised himself up. He moved to Dag's face, brushed his nose against her cheek, and ever so politely—though a bit out of breath—asked in her ear, "Dag, can I fuck you?" She looked at him, a bit wild-eyed, and simply said, "Yes."

He stripped off his jeans, reached into his back pocket for a condom, and tore it open. He knelt in front of her, rolled it onto his swollen cock, and stroked the tip of it against her moist opening. She breathed deeply—not reluctant, but nervous, if I was reading her right. Dag had told me about when she'd lost her virginity with another woman; obviously it had been nothing like this. While I could see a question passing over her face, I could tell she was hungry to feel him inside her. She pushed upward toward him and he slid home easily against the slickness he had left on her with his mouth, coaxed out of her with his tongue. Dag let out a moan.

Rob didn't waste any time—meeting no resistance he began to fuck her deep and long, pulling almost all the way out before ramming back into her willing cunt again. She met his strokes with her own, and before long they were two bodies pulling and grunting and sweating. I was crushed against the headboard by Dag's back; all I could do was watch them and crave to be closer somehow. Their nakedness was right in front of me but tantalizingly out of reach.

It was a violent dance, a hard rutting; Dag's strong hands gripped Rob's ass and slammed him into her, and Rob clenched his teeth and hammered her as though he were an animal in heat. As Dag began again to moan, she grabbed him by the jaw and started talking. "That's it, fuck me hard, bitch. I'm telling you to fuck me harder." Hearing that seemed to crank Rob up another notch. Dag let out a strangled yell and began to convulse against him, and Rob gave two last hard thrusts and choked on a cry of his own, his face twisted in ecstasy as he orgasmed in Dag's pulsing cunt.

Rob collapsed onto Dag's chest, his arms trembling, and Dag hooked her ankles around his knees and held him close. The world was still for a moment, just breathing and heartbeats and our dizzy coming down. Then Dag reached up to tenderly stroke the side of Rob's face. "If you don't mind," she said quietly, "I have something to attend to."

Rob slipped his softening cock out of her and rolled to the side, his chest still heaving. Dag sat up, and I finally took a full breath after being pinned by their weight. Dag turned over onto her stomach and, finally, happily for me, slipped two fingers into me and began to flick her tongue over my long-swollen clit. I was on the edge of a come already, and when Rob opened his eyes, he scooted over to me and slipped one of his own fingers alongside Dag's palm and gradually into me, then a second one. They moved inside me in tandem, stretching me open. The intensity of the combined penetration, along with Dag's skilled tongue and the sudden shock of Rob's thumb pressing into my asshole brought me to an explosive orgasm, waves of heat crashing over my body as the two beautiful boys worked my pleasure.

When I'd stopped coming, Dag pulled me down and wrapped her arms around my waist, holding me close. We could barely move. Rob slid off the bed and trotted out of the room, reappearing a few seconds later with the bowl of grapes. He lay on his side and fed us each the cool, juicy fruits one by one, while Dag brushed her hand back and forth over his shoulder blade. She trailed her finger down his spine, and he shivered, arching up to her touch like a cat being petted. He looked up at her shyly, and Dag caught his eye, then grinned down at me.

"The night is still young," she said with a wink.

THE HALL OF JUSTICE

Sloane Square

I was bad last night. Really bad.

For months I've been wanting to get my hands on him. He was young, tender. Not a virgin, I hoped. I knew he wanted me too, but there was another woman.

It was Halloween.

I let him warm up with a couple of drinks, then I sat close to him with my hand on his knee. It took two minutes for him to get up his courage.

His mouth was on mine forcefully, his tongue strong. I was surprised by his aggressiveness. God, how I wanted to climb on top of him, but that other woman was a distraction.

We pulled away from each other, panting. I took a sip of my drink and smiled at him.

I exhaled. "Baby, that was good."

Justin seemed pleased. I was dying to wrap my legs around him, but there were so many fucking people around.

My friends were looking at me.

One of them mouthed, "What are you doing?"

I slid next to my friend and whispered, "You know I want to break him in."

"What about her?"

"Maybe I'll have them both."

We grinned at each other.

Another round of drinks went down easily. Justin and I moved to the dance floor.

Everywhere shirtless men were pressed against each other. The music was pounding. The gin had gone to my head, but I was already drunk on power.

There was a woman in a latex catsuit. Her nipples were jutting through the slick fabric. It was hypnotizing. There was a man in a leather mask, his torso covered with tattoos; and five beautiful men in drag, dressed as the Fanta Girls, their long, long legs smooth in stockings and high heels. I wanted to look under their skirts.

We were dancing, the bass thundering through us. Justin was still distracted by the other woman. She looked so prim, so buttoned up, adrift.

The slick bodies surrounded us. Two, three, four men gripping each other; chests, arms, hands in dark places.

I put my hands on her hips and pulled her toward me. She did not resist. Her eyes were shining, wet. I looked at Justin. He was breathing deeply through his mouth. I began to unbutton her shirt, first from the bottom exposing her smooth stomach, and then at her creamy neck. I yanked the elastic from her hair and shook the waves around her face. Her hands slid around my waist and then our lips touched, with a jolt. Her mouth was open and I slid inside. The lights were flashing behind my eyes. I could smell her perfume and my own. Her body was tight against me.

I opened my eyes. Catwoman was whipping one of my

friends. Even through the strobe lights I could tell he was hard.

I found Justin. He was standing in the midst of the surging tide. He stumbled forward. The other woman was still in my arms. I pulled her against me as he stepped in behind her. His mouth was on mine in a frenzy. His fingers, searing, dug into my shoulders as we crushed her between us. Her head was flung back, mouth open, as we three writhed to the music. My fingers found his pants pocket and I delved inside to feel him. Her hungry sex was pressed against mine and I felt like I was having them both.

My senses were on overload. I remembered a report I did in school. Pick one of the five senses. Only five? The sixth sense must be when you know you're dripping wet. The seventh is when you feel your cock stiffen. The eighth...

I looked up. There was a pretty boy dressed as Wonder Woman adjusting his breastplate. I hoped she would use the Golden Lariat on us.

I was tired of waiting. I took Justin's hand and led him off the dance floor.

There was a naughty schoolgirl dancing on the platform. She could have used a spanking.

He was following me blindly, weaving in and out of the groping hands, the thrusting bodies.

I couldn't wait another minute to be alone with him. I pushed open the door to the Ladies' Room. It smelled like sex. Had I been a man, I would have been instantly hard.

I felt like I was entering a new dimension. Boys, girls, boys dressed as girls, girls who had been boys.

Justin was gripping my hand. His eyes blinking, without seeing. The music was loud, the voices blaring.

I pushed him into one of the stalls. We were rough. My back

was against the door. I was pinned in place by his insistent hard-on.

Suddenly I dropped to my knees. Justin gasped and steadied himself, forehead pressed against the door. I yanked open his belt.

"Oh Jesus!"

Was that fear in his voice? Or excitement?

"You're not a virgin, are you, baby?"

"No, but it's been a long..."

He shuddered as I took him deep in my mouth. I could barely hear him moan over the clamor in the room.

I glared up at him. His mouth was agape. His eyes were wide, then narrowed to slits, then wide again. Each time he opened them he seemed surprised to see me there. He dropped one hand to touch my hair, bracing himself with the other as I slammed him into my wet mouth. My hands were on his hips, directing the rhythm.

Someone was smoking a joint. The thick perfume hung in waves around us. Justin pulled me to my feet, his hands digging down the front of my pants. Through the din, I tried to hear the *pop-pop-pop* of the button-fly. He jumped as if stung when his fingers told him I had gone commando.

"Oh baby, I forgot to wear panties." My voice was dripping.

He nodded. His response choked in his throat. His right hand delved between my legs. With his left, he eased my jeans over my hips. He had been a pianist and his finger work was still good.

We were both panting. There was a racket from the next stall. A few girls had gone in together. I figured they were doing lines or dropping X. The whole room was alive with scents and murmurs. I hoped people were getting off in all the other stalls. I didn't bother to stifle the sounds of our action as his slick fingers played furiously.

I pushed him onto the toilet seat. His pants were at his knees, legs spread as wide as the fabric would allow. His pulsing sex beckoned. I climbed on top, straddling him. He was pushing my shirt up to get at my breasts.

There was a small opening between the sides of the stall and the wall. I slipped my fingers in and, gripping tightly, began to ride and rut. Juice was pouring over him. My biceps were shaking from the exertion. I had superhuman strength. I was hurtling through space and time.

Each time I thrust against him, his head would slam into the metal seat-cover dispenser. Justin didn't seem to notice. I thought I could rip the walls off the stall like some Incredible Hulk, pumped up on hormones.

"I am so fucking hot for you, baby!"

"You're, you're..." His head was banging against the holder.

"I think we should become lovers." I felt like a rodeo cowboy, bucking. "I mean regular, frequent lovers."

From the next stall someone was touching my fingers.

Justin was breathless. His long lashes fluttered against his cheek.

I put my hand behind his head to soften the blows. This would be a shitty time for him to get a concussion.

I continued at full gallop.

"Maybe even the three of us," I mused.

His body tensed and I was thrown high, suspended mid-lunge. The clock stopped.

Had I stayed on for eight seconds?

We crashed down together.

The finish line was in sight and I could hear a roar from the stands. I was cheering with them at the top of my lungs. It seemed like everyone in the room was rooting for me.

THE IMPORTANCE OF GOOD NETWORKING

Saskia Walker

The importance of good networking became intimately apparent to me when I got to grips with Carl Sedgemore, our new IT man. In fact Carl hammered the fundamentals of good networking home with such exquisite attention to detail that I was thoroughly fascinated. It's his specialist subject, and the day he arrived in our offices he became mine.

Belinda informed me of his presence that first day. She walked back into our cube, leaned over my monitor and mouthed "Fresh meat" at me, nodding her head beyond the next cube.

Fresh meat? My radar was immediately up and tuning in to nearby conversations. Our open-plan, cube-divided office space was such that you could pick it up or tune it out at will. "Where?"

"Three cubes thataway. New IT bloke designated to our floor." A smug, knowing smile lifted her mouth as she turned back to her PC.

I didn't bother to hide my curiosity; Belinda had known me

for five years. Geeky, intelligent guys really did it for me. I was busting to see this bloke and check out the fresh meat for myself. I ran my fingers through my hair and stood up, glancing casually across the cubes as I did so. I could see Dave Chatham, the IT manager for the whole building, talking to someone, but alas the other person was sitting down. A full-on reconnaissance mission was required. Snatching up the outgoing documents from my mail tray I shimmied my skirt straight, smoothing it over my hips, and headed out of our cube.

Dave's head swiveled as I approached and I smiled over the cube wall, my glance going to the other guy. He had shaggy, black hair, long to his neck and unruly. He wore glasses with thin black frames. Deliciously geeky. He'd made an effort with his appearance, but he was barely passable for a business environment. I could see the creases in his brand-new shirt. His tie wasn't quite done up properly. Lean and uncomfortable as he appeared in his office clothes, my guess was he was fresh out of college. When I got to the entrance to his cube, I dropped my mail on the floor.

Both Dave and the new guy turned to watch as I bent to retrieve the envelopes. The new guy was riveted. He pushed his glasses up the bridge of his nose, revealing a wrist wound with thin, black leather twines—a bit of an alternative edge, perhaps? I had a sudden image of him playing guitar. As I stood up I rearranged my clothes and smiled over at the pair of them, apologizing for interrupting. That's how I got my introduction.

I soon learned more about Carl. He was single, fresh out of college as I had thought, and a real computer whiz in both software and hardware. He knew computer systems inside out and, apparently, what this bloke didn't know about computer networks wasn't worth knowing. That information came from the more explicit networking resource of the office—gossip.

So I decided to go after him. No guarantees he would bite, but I was reasonably presentable and it sure as hell livens up the job trying. He was attractive in a subtle, bohemian way and the thought of getting to him turned me on. Part of it was the intelligence; part of it was the sexual thrill of coming on to him. It's the look of shock, the complete look of awe that this type of man gives when presented with a dominant woman in his space.

When I had the chance to chat with him by the coffee machine, I asked him if he would explain networking to me. "Just as a personal favor," I added, smiling. Of course I knew about networking; I had a taste for this kind of man, after all. No, something about listening to a bloke speak enthusiastically on the virtues of his chosen field gets me sexually aroused.

"Sure thing," he replied. He looked surprised but launched into his area of expertise with ease. I listened to him talking about harnessing the individual power of an intelligent unit and realizing the power of teamwork in computer terms, and my body was humming. Between my thighs, I was getting hotter all the time. There'd been two other men like this in my life, a French exchange student I met at college who could talk about metaphysics all night long, and a guy I'd dated for a year while he talked about software design. Both were intense, intelligent men. Like Carl. Watching Carl's green eyes flicker as he talked, I noticed how long his fingers were, wrapped around his coffee cup; how stark his cheekbones. I wanted to feed him. I wanted to fuck him.

"At the present time, the ultimate network is the Internet," he continued, "but who knows what the future holds." His eyes glittered with enthusiasm.

I set my coffee cup down and fanned myself lightly with the printed report in my hand.

"Sorry," he said, noticing me shifting from one foot to the other. "That's a bit technical and probably not what you meant."

He was definitely the kind of man I went for, geeky and not quite sure of himself outside his chosen field. I wanted to be the one to make him sure.

"That's exactly what I meant. Thanks Carl. I hope you don't mind me asking, but do you play guitar?"

He looked surprised. "Yes, how did you know?"

I reached out and touched his fingers. "Your hands." Electricity raced between us. The surface of the coffee in the cup he held rippled, tension beading up in it. "I hope we get to chat again soon, I enjoyed it."

"Yes, that would be good," he said, pushing his glasses up the bridge of his nose with his free hand. I glanced back as I walked away and noticed that he was admiring my stacked heels. I made a mental note of that.

I plotted my moves and waited until Belinda was away for a training day and I had the cube to myself. I'd planned in advance, wearing a low-cut top and short skirt, my highest heels and my sexiest underwear to give me confidence.

His eyes nearly popped out of their sockets when I appeared at his cube wall. I rested my elbows on it, leaning my boobs on top of the ledge. "Hi, Carl. I hope I'm not interrupting. I've got a problem with my mouse."

I could tell he was trying desperately to prize his gaze away from my chest area. Smiling, I leaned further forward, my boobs spilling out of my top. "Do I have to fill in a form to get your attention?"

"No, definitely not." He grinned and clutched at the edge of his desk as he stood up. "It probably just needs a new part. I'll check it out now."

Perfect.

He followed close behind me and as we wended our way back to my cube I felt his eyes boring into me. I gestured at the desk. He sat in my chair. I put my hands on his shoulders, stood behind him and peered at the computer alongside him. I could feel his shoulders grow taut under my hands. The sexual tension was ratcheting up with every moment. He blinked several times before continuing. He was a loaded weapon about to blow.

Wriggling the mouse, he shook his head. "Yup, it's dead. I've got a batch of spares back in my cube. I'll fetch one now." Reluctantly, he stood up, one finger adjusting his collar as he glanced over me again.

Oh, the sweet combination of arousal and discomfort was too good. "You're the expert, but I should probably mention it happened before and Belinda found the connector had dislodged." This time I'd ensured that the connector had dislodged. "Maybe you should check that first?"

"I guess I should," he replied, while his eyes dropped to the floor. He was staring at my shoes and feet in a kind of mesmerized trance.

After a moment, I gestured under the desk with a smile. He got down on his hands and knees, giving me a look at his tight buttocks. Nice. When he crawled under the desk, I sat back down in the chair, trapping him in there.

Leaning down, I flashed him an eyeful of cleavage. "Take your time," I murmured.

He shuffled around and his whole body jolted when he caught sight of me. His head whacked the underside the desk and it shuddered. "Shit. I mean, sorry."

I bit my lip, containing my urge to chuckle. "Is it okay if I sit here while you are underneath...?"

"Yes...please do."

I sat back, easing the chair in and shifting my legs nearer him. Even through my stockings, I could feel his breath hot on my skin. I had got him well and truly trapped. Rubbing one calf with the toe of the other foot, I noticed that it was very quiet under there. It was working. I moved my legs into different positions, sometimes brushing against him. Not a sound or a move came from underneath the desk, but the intense heat welling from under there was the signal I needed. Taking a deep breath, I pushed my swivel chair back, lifted one stacked heel up and pivoted it on the edge of my desk, flashing the underside of my thigh and stocking tops at him.

He was scrunched in the same position, his eyes glazed as he stared up at me in disbelief. He didn't look like he was trying to go anywhere in a hurry, in fact he hadn't budged since I'd sat down.

My pulse was racing. "Is it okay down there for you, Carl?"

He gave a hoarse laugh. "Yes, I'm um...just admiring the view."

Brave. And now that he'd bitten, it was all systems go. Our very own network was up and running. "You can touch me if you want to." I could hear voices in the distance outside the cube, but they were fast zoning out, my attention fully harnessed.

With hardly a second's hesitation, one hand reached for me, but it was the foot still on the floor he went for. Stroking it with his fingers, he moved slowly over it, then under its arch and around its heel. With tentative fingers, he stroked the top of my foot with such adoration that my head dropped back and my hands gripped the arms of my chair. I'd hit gold! The man was a pure sensualist. He slipped his fingers around the back of my ankle and lowered his head to kiss the toe of my shoe. What a rush! Sensation shot the length of my leg; my pussy prickled with anxiety, needy for contact. I had to hold tight to stop from squirming in my seat.

He ran his mouth up my shin, and then kissed my knee. Using both hands, he stroked my inner thighs, reverently embracing my stocking tops. I was starting to tremble. Tension and

need thrummed just inches from his hands, and he was closing. I watched the glossy surface of his hair as he moved in. He
stroked one finger down the surface of my panties, pushing it
into the groove of my pussy, tantalizing my clit. I gasped aloud.
My foot skidded against the desk, my right leg twitched and
bounced against him. I was about to urge him on, desperately,
when he snuck a finger down one side of the fabric and thrust
it underneath.

I heard him groan and saw him shuffle, and then I grew light-
headed when he moved the pad of his finger into my groove,
more fingertips following. My eyes clamped shut. He paddled
his fingers against me, maddening my clit and the sensitive folds
surrounding it. The contact was too good. My hips were rolling
into him and he worked me harder, each of his fingers moving independently. *Like strumming a guitar.* The thought echoed
through my mind as a sweet, sudden orgasm hit me.

I heard his voice in the distance. Opening my eyes, and I saw
him smiling up at me from between my open legs. "I said I better
get back to my desk now, but...um, perhaps we could go for a
drink after work?"

I pulled myself together. "Yes, I'd love to go for a drink. I
have to work until six, why don't I come over to you when I'm
done?" An idea was already ticking over in my mind. "Could
you plug my mouse back in before you go?" I winked.

He stared at me for several moments until recognition regis-
tered in his expression. "You did that to get me down here?"

"It was all that talk about networking." I could tell he
thought I was joking. *Little did he know.*

He ducked back under the desk and I stood up, letting him
emerge without further hindrance. As he did, he adjusted the
bulge in his pants.

I snatched at his wrist, holding his hand on his cock. "I'll help you with that when I come over to your cube, later." I wanted to see what he had in his pants soon; we could go for the drink afterward.

"I can hardly wait," he replied, pushing his glasses up his nose with his free hand. His eyes were glazed; he was in a bad way.

Power rushed in my veins. "I'll send you a message every hour from now until then, just to be sure that you don't forget I'm coming."

His eyes flashed shut. I felt his hand tighten on his cock. I moved away when I heard voices passing and he grabbed a file to cover his crotch—practical and quick-witted too.

Once an hour I sent him a message, questioning him about male-to-female connectors and spare parts. His replies assured me he would be pleased to look into any needs I had as soon as humanly possible. I couldn't help touching myself under the desk, thrilled that my scheme had worked. My pussy was heavy and sensitive from the orgasm he'd given me, my cunt aching for more. He was good with his hands, his attention to feet and shoes an unexpected bonus. Each time I sent him an email I thanked him for his kind attentions and told him how much it was appreciated. I felt his responses in his words coming over the network and in the atmosphere across the office. The clock ticked on, arousal building with every moment.

At five past six, the only other person around was the cleaner, who was vacuuming each cube starting on the far side. I shut down my documents, grabbed my bag and headed over to Carl's cube.

He grinned when I leaned over the wall. "Hello," he said and eased his chair out from the desk.

I stared pointedly at his crotch then sidled into the cube. "We're all alone here apart from the cleaner. She won't get over here for ages." I bent over him, my hands on the arms of his chair, trapping him in it, and kissed him on the mouth. His body was rigid and he moaned under me. "I've been hot for more ever since this morning," I said as I pulled back. Glancing down at his crotch I could see that his bulge had gotten bigger. Reaching for his belt I looked him in the eye. "I want to sit on your cock."

I thought his eyes would pop out of his head. He about managed to nod, fumbling with his fly, helping me. His dick bounced out. "I've been hard most of the afternoon," he muttered. "Seeing you come, earlier," he added, as if he needed an explanation.

I leaned over him and then reached for the condom packet I'd tucked into my cleavage.

"Man, that is so hot," he groaned as I pulled it out.

"I thought you might like it." I chuckled and then bent to run my tongue over the head of his cock. He shuddered vigorously, his hands clutching at the arms of his chair. I rolled the condom down the length of him. "I'm going to grind your cock until you come, right here and right now."

He gave a soft, disbelieving laugh, lifting his hands in the air nonchalantly before clutching at the arms of the chair again. "Feel free."

I pulled my skirt up and he stared, wide-eyed. I'd taken my panties off this time. I turned around and forced his legs shut with my knees, straddling them, my skirt up around my waist. Behind me I heard him cursing under his breath.

"Oh, I'm doing this on one condition," I said over my shoulder. "You've got to talk dirty to me."

The look on his face was priceless. "Dirty?"

I nodded. "Tell me about networks again, Carl. Tell me about plugging into the central supply, tell me about system routing." I winked over my shoulder and lowered myself down, guiding his cock inside me.

"That's so good," he moaned, as I drove myself down on to him. Each time I lifted up higher to thrust deeper again, I could see the cleaner on the far side of the office going about her business, oblivious to what we were up to. *Ah, the network of intrigue that can exist in open-plan offices.*

"Tell me, Carl."

"Jesus, I thought you were kidding."

I squeezed his cock tight, grinding my hips. "Oh no, I wasn't kidding. It really turns me on."

"Networking is...essential...for a company to function at... full capacity." He staggered his way through the sentence, his fingers biting into my buttocks.

"Oh that's good." Leaning forward, I clutched the edge of his desk and then began to pump. His cock felt good, rock hard and burning hot from waiting. I rode it, squeezing it tight and milking every drop of pleasure out of him. "Go on."

"It maximizes...return, by using all available...power...re-sources as and when needed."

When I lifted up, he moaned behind me mumbling something about how good it looked. My cunt started melting and my knuckles went white as I gripped on to the table.

"Key basic factors include"—he groaned—"accurate server configuration."

I was close to coming, and then I noticed movement at the periphery of my vision. "The cleaner's on her way over, hurry," I blurted, anxiety hitting me. We were both so close, I didn't even know if I could stop. I didn't have to think about it for long, because suddenly my view shifted and my feet left the floor. Carl shoved me bodily over his desk. My breasts were crushed on the surface; my hands clutching at handfuls of paperwork, bits of hard drive and other computer gear on the desk as I grappled for purchase.

He leaned over my back, his cock still wedged deep and getting deeper still as he banged into me. "A solid, working network ensures no loss of packets in transfer," he said against my ear, with a hoarse laugh.

That was too good! My cunt was on fire, my cervix crushed and throbbing. I moaned and bit on my wrist as I came, my body spasming uncontrollably, release flooding me. "Do you think this...network...is secure enough?" I urged him on to his completion, my lips drawn back as hot wave upon wave of pleasure shot through my cunt.

"We're about to find out." He wedged himself deeper, lifting my hips from the desk, and shot his load.

With a show of efficiency and nonchalance that stunned me, he rocked back into the chair, lifting me bodily to my feet, and pulled my skirt down around my hips. By the time the cleaner appeared by his cube, he'd zipped up, straightened my skirt and was leading me through a network directory on his screen.

"Good networking is the key to quality IT systems. An international organization such as ours would be useless without one." He waved at the cleaner as she passed by and then stopped me swaying with one hand. "Now, how about that drink?"

I nodded, laughing, and rested against the edge of the desk to steady myself. I needed that drink, just like I needed a good IT man. I leaned over and kissed him on the mouth, my fingers meshing in his hair. I savored that kiss and so did he, meeting it openly, his tongue tasting me slowly, reverently.

"Can we do this again?" I asked when we drew back.

He nodded and slipped his hand between my thighs, stroked my damp flesh, applying pressure in all the right places. His thumb resting on my oversensitive clit was too good. "A good network needs regular maintenance," he replied, one eyebrow lifting.

I think I fell in love with him in that moment. "In that case, it's a good job I've found me such an expert," I replied, and pulled him into my arms.

COFFEE SHOP BOY

A. D. R. Forte

Coffee Shop: Her

Yeah, I stare. I stare, hoping he's just a little bit freaked out. He knows he's hot, that he gets stares from the fags to the hags and everybody else in between. Even if he'll never let on that he notices the attention and likes it.

He's the consummate secret-fantasy slut. And I'm not above that bandwagon.

He comes in every morning, sometimes at lunch. And it's either latte or a cup of the extra-rich brew. Cream, no sugar. Yup, that about describes him to a T. Not a hint of sweet in his walk, his designer polo shirts and flat-front trousers, ubiquitous Pocket PC/phone at his hip.

He gets his liquid fix, gets a napkin sometimes if the counter guy's dribbled coffee down the side of the cup. He takes a sip, maybe two, and then he's out the door and off to conquer the world. No wasted time. No lingering over the paper in an armchair and staring at the college girls like his fellow yuppies. Nope. This boy's got a purpose.

My downstairs neighbor works at his firm, and she gives me the skinny. Not that there's much to give. He's a bit of an ass, she tells me over pasta and a bottle of cheap wine as we sit in my living room painting our toenails blood purple.

"Don't know why you're so interested in him. Guys like that last about five seconds."

"Peh! I can make him last as long I want."

I'm confident in that boast. I have a weakness for taking an uptight, intellectual nazi or a clean-cut prep-boy and turning him into a dirty, sweaty, inhibition-free fuck toy.

Hey, I want to do my bit for humanity and make the world a better place too. And I'm damned good at it.

So I tell Stefany, "Give me one night with him. Betcha he'll call in sick the next day."

"Not a chance." She shakes her head and slurps up a mouthful of spaghetti. "Never does. And if he's not there, he calls ten times to check on his team. I'm so fucking glad I don't work in that department."

I'm not deterred. "Well what else do you know about him? What's his fetish?"

She shrugs, purses her lips, shakes her head. "No idea. Told you, he does nada for me so I haven't paid attention." She pauses, thinking.

"Oh, he likes jazz."

"Jazz?"

She giggles at my wide-eyed disbelief.

"Yep. Boney James, Gerald Albright; that kinda thing. Has a ton of modern art and sculpture stuff in his office. Pretentious little fruitcake."

This from Stefany, who considers manga the be-all and

end-all of artistic expression and everything else "pretentious fruitcake." But I'm having a hell of a time trying to get my head around the idea of Coffee Shop Boy having a sensuous side. It doesn't quite add up, and I'm still sitting there with my mouth open while Stefany sips her wine and looks at me with her head tilted to the side.

"You'll pretty much scare the shit out of him," she says.

At work I think about Stefany's comment and chuckle. Tonight I'm trying to determine cause of death for a crack addict: all bone and skin. The body almost looks like a modern sculpture. It's hard to decide on homicide or overdose with what I'm looking at, a matter of interpretation. Much like with art.

I wonder if Coffee Shop Boy would see the humor in that comparison. Probably not. But that just makes me want him more.

After work, Evan and I wash our hands, hang up scrubs and lab coats, and head for Barista Bob's.

"Juicy java. That's what I need," Evan says, looking at the menu as we stand in line. He's not talking about coffee of course. My lab assistant spends most every night lamenting the dearth of romantic liaisons in his life.

"You need to get laid," I reply.

"You volunteering?"

I snort. "You couldn't handle it, babe. I'd have you screaming for your mommy in about a minute."

Evan folds his arms and pouts.

"Yeah, I probably would, knowing you. Kink Queen."

"Guilty as charged."

As I shrug I catch the sound of stifled laughter behind us; Evan and I aren't exactly the most soft-spoken people. I turn.

And he's standing right there, not even a foot away; the closest I've ever been to him. He smells like Givenchy Blue and his hair is still just a little wet from his morning shower. A copy of *Barron's* is tucked under his arm—light reading I'm sure—and he's smiling, thoroughly amused from his eavesdropping.

What else can I do? I smile right back.

I extend my hand, Champagne and Strawberries soft, showing no trace of last night's work. He takes it. Strong, unhesitating Wall Street grip. He makes eye contact and I meet him gaze for gaze.

"Good morning, I'm the Kink Queen. Pleasure to meet you," I say.

At that he laughs outright, and I don't care what Stefany thinks: this man could make a woman melt if he wanted to. Using nothing but that laugh.

"I'm honored," he says.

He keeps hold of my hand just a fraction longer, and then Evan's finished ordering. I release him and turn away. Just a silly, random moment between strangers. But even as I order and move on down the line, as he moves forward to get his Hawaiian blend, I'm thinking about that moment of touch. Thinking about that laugh.

Evan and I are sitting at a window table when he begins to leave. Some part of me hopes that this morning he'll break his routine and walk over, curious to see what a random moment can become, given a chance. Now that I've put the ball in his court.

But he doesn't.

I sip my espresso and frown. I'm defeated, yet I can't help following him with my gaze just as I always do. Knowing he's fully aware of my stare, even though he never once looks in the direction of our table.

He gets a napkin this morning; folds it, wraps it around his cup, starts toward the door. And then just as he pushes the door open, he stops. He turns and meets my gaze over the heads of all the caffeine lovers and strangers between us. Half a smile; that's all he concedes. And then he's off to conquer again.

Office: Him

I shut my office door and put the coffee cup on the desk. I'm thinking about her eyes. They remind me of a storm. When she looks at me I can feel the hair on the back of my neck rise, the tingle of electricity snake its way down my spine.

I sink into my chair and drag my cup toward me. I figure I have maybe a half hour before my boss or one of my team bursts in here with a catastrophe. If I had my choice, I'd want her here, in the office. On the desk.

I'd slide that sensible black pencil skirt up over her knees and her hips. Hold her wrists out of the way so she can't distract me with her touch. I wonder if she's a shave-it-all type of girl. I imagine her that way. Because I like the idea of nothing between her skin and my mouth.

I'd lick her exposed clit. Lick her until she was wet and so aroused it hurt and she insisted I stop. I'd stop. But I'd give her light barely-there kisses to torment her even worse. Kiss the sides of her slit and her mound, down to her ass. Blow gently on her flushed, glistening clit and listen to her moan.

I can tell she's the kind of woman who likes to be in control. So I want to hear her elegant, sarcastic voice gone breathless and soft. I want her helpless to resist her own desire.

I sip my coffee. Wish I was tasting her instead. My cock is hard; has been for the last ten minutes. I sigh and reach for my laptop. I have work to do and I can't spend all day fantasizing about fucking some girl from the coffee shop.

But I wish I could.

Damned 7:30 a.m. meeting on Wednesday. I don't get to Bob's until well after lunch and of course she's gone by then. I try not to be disappointed. But on Thursday and Friday I'm there bright and early.

She isn't.

On Monday, it gets to me. The pale twerp she usually comes in with is at a table by himself and I walk over.

"Hey."

He looks up from his paper and recognizes me. Gives me a "Hey, what's goin' on?"

I nod at the empty seat across from him.

"I haven't seen her all week. Is she okay?"

He nods. "Yeah, she's just working. Been hectic this week and she's been pulling doubles."

I nod. I should tell him to say I miss her, that I said hi.

But I don't; I just say, "Wow that's gotta suck. Well, take care." I reason that he probably wouldn't give her the message anyway; he's looking at me like I've stepped on his toes. Maybe I have. Good.

I give him a slap on the shoulder and leave.

Finally, on Friday morning, I'm given a reprieve. She's at her table by the window, but she's focused on the oversized folder of documents and papers stacked before her. The twerp is rubbing her feet and I'm insanely jealous. How the hell does *he* get to rub her feet? But with those gargantuan, chunky-soled shoes she likes to wear kicked off, I see for the first time that she has delicate feet. Slender, pretty, girly feet.

She rubs a tired hand over her eyes and reaches for her coffee, still looking at her paperwork. Twerp says something, she replies and frowns, sips her coffee. She makes a disgusted face and takes another few rapid sips. I figure the coffee's probably cold.

At the counter I ask Bob what she's having. He knows the regulars, and doesn't even have to think about it.

"Espresso with whipped cream and caramel drizzle," he tells me.

"Get me one of those too."

He winks and obliges.

I walk up behind her and reach over her right shoulder to put the cup within her reach.

"You looked like you could use a refill," I say.

She turns to look up at me. Her eyes are shadowed with dark circles that have nothing to do with eyeliner, her lipstick's faded out and the elf braids in her hair are coming loose and untidy. She's never looked more stunning.

"Thanks." She reaches up to squeeze my outstretched arm, and her voice is soft with surprise and tiredness. From my vantage point, through the tangle of mesh sweater, shirt and bustier, I can see a soft, unmistakable curve. And all the blood rushes from my head. I can't move. Or think.

"It *is* just what I needed."

"You're welcome." Automatic response because I still can't think, and her touch on my arm is making this oh so much worse.

I straighten up and she releases me, smiling. I refuse to think about what I want to do to her. Not now. Not a chance in hell, pretty girl. You're not winning this one.

I rest one hand on her shoulder and lean down so that she can feel my breath on her neck when I speak.

"Don't work too hard," I say as I rub the muscles between neck and shoulder. I feel her inhale sharply and I smile, because I love the sound of that involuntary breath. And because twerp is now glaring at me with pure, disgusted envy.

"I won't," she says. Her voice shakes, just that little bit, even though she tries to cover it up.

I give her a last squeeze, a last smile. Then I escape. And her gaze follows me all the way to the door.

Apartment: Her
Timing is everything. So of course, mine sucks shit. I get back to the apartment Friday afternoon and fall into bed fully dressed. I'm exhausted.

Maybe it was a good thing the DA's office decided to have a political disaster on their hands with that case. A few days without seeing me seems to have made Coffee Shop Boy realize that I might slip through his fingers, and I don't think he likes the idea. Not if today was any indication.

I can still feel the warmth of his hand. I want to buy a bottle of Givenchy and soak my sheets in it so I can close my eyes and smell him while I get off. No, I'll just get *him* soaked into my sheets. That's what I really want.

But like I said, my timing is shit. I can feel the sticky, sore sniffles that herald a cold. No way am I going anywhere if I'm sick. Not even for *him*. And I'm so goddamned tired; my eyelids are giving out on me.

I fall into dreams of Coffee Shop Boy.

I'm sick all weekend and into the next week. Great way to burn up vacation time, that. When Evan and I finally get to Bob's at midmorning on Wednesday, I still feel crappy. And pissy. After a night of wrestling with uncooperative cadavers, I smell like the chemical factory of some Batman villain. I hope to god Coffee Shop Boy's not there. And he isn't.

Evan points out the fact with a triumphant air. Jealous twit. So I tell him to fuck off and go to the counter. But Bob has a surprise for me.

"Wait! Hang on a sec," he says as I get my order. He finishes ringing up a customer and proceeds to fumble around behind the register while I wait, sniffing and scowling. I'm about to walk away when he produces a sealed business envelope and hands it over.

"This was left for you."

My name is scribbled on it in Bob's handwriting, but my heart starts going a mile a minute, and not from caffeine either. Who else would leave me anything here? I thank Bob and rush to the table. Inside the envelope there's a single sheet of notepad paper.

> Hi. Heard you're on vacation and I have to go out of town the rest of the week. But I'd love to see you Saturday. Around 3. Near the angel statue at the cemetery? Either way I'll be there. Hope I see you.

Now *that* was what a love letter should be. Fuck pansy sonnets and floral metaphors. In only four lines, he'd gotten my panties wet. He hadn't signed it; he didn't have to.

"Date?" Evan asks, sitting down opposite me.

"Bet your ass."

Evan shakes his head. "I don't know how you do it."

I don't either. But it works.

Cemetery

He's sitting on a bench, Pocket PC in hand. As always, he's in slacks and polo shirt. But today the weather's worthy of a Monet painting and, just to confuse him, I've gone for the Innocente look: white skirt flowing to my ankles, amber beads, my hair pulled back in a simple bun. But my tank top shows the danse macabre tattoo spiraling around my left arm, the alchemist skull with its blood-hued rose on my right shoulder. He looks up, takes it all in as I stand before him, waiting for him to choose.

He puts the Pocket PC down and reaches for my right hand with his left. Never taking his eyes from my face, he brings my wrist to his lips. Lips that are so hot, so knowing on my skin. And Stefany was *so* wrong. This boy isn't one bit scared.

I sit beside him on the bench and nod at the Pocket PC.

"Not working are you?"

He smiles and shakes his head.

"Not a chance. Reading."

He holds it out for me to see and I peer at the screen.

"Vampire novel?"

He shrugs. "Guilty pleasure."

I laugh loud enough to startle a handful of nearby crows. "Do you have a lot of those?"

He leans back on the bench and smiles, answers in a tone that is not his businessman's voice. "No, just a very, very select few."

He reaches out and traces the skeletal figures on my arm, bony hands joined in glee all the way up to my shoulder. But his fingers don't stop where the tattoo ends. They go on, up to my neck.

"I want to let your hair down," he says.

I nod. I can't refuse.

Any other day, with any other man I would say no just to make him beg. But today, from this man, it isn't a request. And all I can do is close my eyes as he unwinds the scarf from around my bun, pulls the hairpins out and drops them in my lap. Tugs at the thick coil until it spills, black as the raven Morrigan's wing, down over my shoulders.

He sticks the Pocket PC in its holder and reaches for me with both hands. He pulls me into his lap. My legs tangle with his and I put my hands on his shoulders for balance, feel him warm and solid and so *close* under my hands. In my grasp. He reaches up to bury his fingers in my hair and plays with it, giving gentle pulls and tugs for a few, innocent seconds. Before he yanks my head down.

No warning and no reprieve. No preamble to let me reconsider.

He isn't kissing to be clever. He isn't kissing to be sweet. He's taking and claiming and using me. I'm his slut, or maybe he's mine. He pulls away from the kiss, breathing hard because my hands are busy caressing the hardness between his legs, and for a moment I think I know just what to expect. But I have no fucking idea. Lightning fast, he catches my wrists, pinions my arms behind my back.

He's pushed the tank top up over my breasts, and I can't move except to squirm and twist while he bends to take my nipples between his teeth. Licking, sucking, biting. Changing to the other just when I can't bear one sensation anymore. Keeping me prisoner all the while. Getting me hotter and wetter by the second, and I wonder if he knows this cotton skirt isn't exactly thick material and he's about to end up with a nice big wet spot on those designer pants of his.

I don't think he cares. He torments me, and I'm almost sobbing with frustrated desire, longing to get his lovely, thick cock in my mouth and return the favor, when he leans back and slides his hands up my arms, loosens his grip. He wraps one arm around my shoulders and gathers my legs into his lap with the other. I figure out what he's trying to do and before I can do more than whisper "Oh hell..." and get my arms around his neck, he stands.

Carrying me like a heroine in a five-dollar romance novel, his conquered prize, he takes me into the shade of the trees. Away from the gaze of casual passersby. He stops on the far side of the angel statue that keeps watch over the grave of some long-decayed city father from two centuries back. I've sat at her feet I don't know how many times. On bad days and good days and simply quiet days.

I've never shared her with a lover until now—and its Coffee Shop Boy of all people. But as he lowers me to the ground and kneels over me, smiling and lifting my damsel-in-distress white skirt up over my hips, I remember that the angel was *his* idea.

Unreal.

I tug at his shirt and he lets me pull it off, along with the T-shirt under it. Powerful shoulders, lightly muscled. I breathe in Givenchy and musky arousal. He takes my tank top off, and a moment later my bra follows.

I see him glance aside and I follow his gaze to my purse and the head scarf carelessly stuffed into the front of it. I'm about to sit up and protest—I see the look in his eyes.

But I don't.

I must be out of my ever-loving mind, but god help me I don't. I raise my hands up and offer them to him. He stares, lips curled in a sarcastic smile. He thought he'd have to fight me, wrestle me every inch of the way to surrender, and instead I'm giving him his victory without a shot fired. And he hates it, but he claims me anyway. He lifts my arms above my head; ties the gold and burnt-orange silk about my wrists.

I feel the gravestone warm and rough under my shoulders and outstretched arms, the tickle of grass at my sides. My skirt is bunched around my waist and he rests on one elbow to trace the shape of the snake curled around my left thigh with its head resting against the lower curve of my belly.

"So beautiful," he says as his fingers pause just below the snake's head. Just above my shaved-bare mound. He meets my gaze and smiles.

"Adorned like a goddess, mystical in her pictures and her secrets," he adds. And I swallow hard. Nobody's ever talked to me that way. How does he know the things I've dreamed of hearing a lover say?

I'm helpless. And it's not because my hands are tied.

He slithers downward and traces my snake with his tongue this time. One hand spreads my legs, opening me to him; the other hand rests on my belly, fingers toying with my navel ring. His tongue flickers between my parted pussy lips and he licks my clit softly at first, pausing to savor my taste. But each lick is a little harder, a little more demanding, and soon I'm sighing and spreading my legs even wider for him. Arching my hips up to give my flesh to his worshipping tongue.

He buries his face in me, moaning, and I feel the vibration of his voice in my clit, in my pussy, in my belly—in my very fucking soul. Here in this place of death where I can still smell the green, living smell of summer; the fertile smell of grass and earth and lovemaking, under the guardian eyes of my stone angel. In this place where death meets life and the circle is completed, I can believe he touches me that intimately. Right now, hell, I can believe in anything.

I close my eyes and die under his mouth. Writhing so hard as I come that I feel the burn of stone bruising my skin. I'm tearing my knuckles and the backs of my hands on the stone of the monument base behind my head as I brace myself and grind against his mouth. I don't care. I'm his bacchante, his willing Persephone. I'm all his.

He doesn't lift himself when he's finished. Only slides upward, between my legs, levers his hands beneath my torso and lifts me up toward him. Rolls us both over so that now I'm on top. I frame his face between my arms, bury my fingers in his hair, kissing him hard. Licking my juices off his chin, off his perfectly trimmed moustache and goatee that define his lips. Lips that have distracted me so often; that today have driven me out of my mind.

I bite his lips and his neck, marking him as mine. But his hands are massaging my bare ass, his fingers are exploring my still-wet pussy, and I want him in me. I want to fill myself with his length, soft and slow. So I ease him in. Teasing.

Half of my teasing is involuntary because I can't find my balance and guide him in with my hands locked together. And he doesn't help, laughing and stroking my hips with light, lazy touches that distract me even more. The silk pulls tight when I angle my hands, painful pressure on my wrists sending numbing tingles through my fingers. But I won't give up. I won't give him the satisfaction of hearing me beg.

And at last I make him prisoner, trap him within me, and I arch backward and up. Grinding the tip of his cock into the most sensitive parts of my pussy; listening to his breath come shallow and hard. The gentle touch of afternoon wind feels like ice on my skin.

Yes, I'm that much on fire.

He reaches up, pulls my hair over one shoulder and tucks it to the side of one breast. He lies there, looking at me with his bruised, bitten lips parted in silent ecstasy while I push down on his chest. Baby-soft hair and skin hot under my palms as I ride him harder. My downstrokes come faster and rougher, and he winces each time I crash into him just a little too hard. He never makes a sound, but he pinches my sore nipples in punishment.

And we hurt each other. Fuck each other. Adore each other.

I've lost count of how often I've come. I want to keep torturing him like this, torturing myself, but my body can only stand so much before it's screaming at me to stop. The muscles in my thighs are trembling with the effort to keep moving.

Has it been five minutes? Or eternity?

I bend forward, running my fingers into his sweat-soaked hair again. I slide up, almost letting him fall out of me. And then down in a rush, like a landslide, like a sudden storm. He gasps and grabs my ass hard. He closes his eyes.

"I want to make you come," I whisper in his ear.

"Never!"

I laugh. Because the spirit is unwilling.

But the flesh is weak.

He fights me, fingers digging into my ass, trying to stop my motion, but I struggle with every last iota of strength. I ride him fast and deep, driving my pussy down the length of his cock, driving him to his limits. Just like he's done to me. Give and take, babe, God and Goddess.

Oh, he fights me. Resists that mounting, maddening pressure in his balls and cock with heroic determination. But he's too far gone and Nature will have her way. He gives in at last, grinding upward, moaning into the skin of my neck. Filling me. And he's mine; my beautiful Hades. He's all mine.

While he unties my hands he gives me kisses. Pillow-soft kisses that steal my air, leave me gasping as if I'm plunging, racing down into the earth, into arms of darkness and stone. I can only stroke my fingers along his cheekbones and smile at him.

He twirls a strand of my hair around his finger. "You scare me, you know that?"

Jazz and vampire novels and sex like skinny-dipping in a midnight thunderstorm. It's a wonder I can manage coherent speech at all, but I hear myself say, "Is that such a bad thing?"

He thinks about it for only a few seconds, gives me a secret smile.

"No. No, it's not bad at all," he replies.

We turn to walk away, back to the world of coffee shops and ordinary things. But he pauses. I see him look up at the angel, my Lady of Death with her stone wings. Then he looks at me, and his gaze is mystery and passion and promise as he takes my hand. I say nothing; I don't ask. Because, after all, I'm just a little freaked out by him, too.

But that's not a bad thing. Not a bad thing at all.

AMERICAN BOTTOM IN LIMOUSIN

Geneva King

Sadie sat fuming in her cell. She hadn't so much as heard a human voice in the last two hours.

"Hello!" she screamed. "Let me out of here! Um, damn. *Laissez-moi...aller d'ici.*" Admittedly not the best French, but hopefully they'd get the gist. "This is inhumane. I'm gonna sue when I get out!" She whacked the bars and flopped on the dingy cot.

"This is so gross," Sadie groaned, trying to touch as little of the fabric as possible. Finally discomfort got the better of her. She balled her sweater beneath her head and curled up.

This was so not in the plan. Nowhere on the itinerary did it say "Get arrested for a crime you didn't commit and get thrown into some horrible decaying French prison." And yet that was exactly what had happened. She didn't speak French well enough to understand what she was being accused of in the first place. And none of her jailers spoke English. She assumed it had something to do with the man selling jewelry. No one had bothered her until he started yelling.

"I'm still in here," she yelled. When there was no answer, she shrugged. Maybe they needed some prodding. *"One hundred bottles of beer on the wall, one hundred bottles of beer. Take one down and pass it around, ninety-nine bottles of beer on the wall...."* She sang loudly in the direction of the guards.

By the time she reached forty-four bottles, Sadie's throat was dry and scratchy. She also needed to pee. Badly. Her cell didn't have a toilet, but she noticed a small drain in the middle of the floor.

"No way am I squatting over that." She sat back on the cot and squeezed her PC muscles together. "It's been a while since I did my Kegels anyhow."

Ten minutes and some frantic prayers later, the cell door opened and a female guard walked in.

Sadie jumped up. *"Madame! Madame! Je m'appelle Sadie et...j'ai...eh* crap...*j'ai besoin de...*bathroom. No, toilet! I need a toilet!"

The woman regarded her with a deadpan expression. She slowly looked Sadie over. Then, to her relief, the guard led her out of the cell and to a small closet.

"Toilette," she grunted.

The bathroom was shabbier than any gas station restroom that Sadie had ever had the misfortune to use, but she accepted it gladly. The guard watched her hover over the seat, but Sadie ignored her.

When she was finished, the lady led her back to the cell. She pushed Sadie inside and locked the door.

"Ma'am! *Madame! Aidez-moi!"*

Sadie slumped back on the bed, working up the desire to finish counting bottles of beer. Fortunately, the woman came back into the room. This time, she was accompanied by a tall, broad-shouldered man.

"You are Sadie Miller?" he asked in accented English. Like that of the female guard, his face didn't display any emotion, or cause for his visit.

"Yes. I want to speak to the American Embassy!" Sadie tried to keep her anger at bay. She didn't want to piss off the only people who would talk to her or even acknowledge her presence. "But first, I want to know why I'm here! I didn't do anything."

He shook his head. "The jewelry man says you stole."

Sadie opened her mouth to argue, but the man cut her off. "I do not come to tell you this. I am here to help you fix the problem. Okay?"

She nodded quickly, pressing against the bars. "I'm listening."

The man gestured to her cot. "Please, sit down." He nodded to his partner and she disappeared, returning with two folding chairs.

"Now Ms. Miller, you want to call the embassy. I do not think that is such a good idea."

Sadie frowned. "Why not?"

He waved his hands around, as if trying to find the right words. "Because they follow rules, they want details. It all gets messy. We want to keep this as clean as possible. *Tu comprends?*"

Sadie nodded slowly, then shook her head. "No, I'm sorry. I don't."

The man sighed. "Ms. Miller, it's very simple. The vendor wants justice. You want this to go away. A few words from me, this problem—gone!" He snapped his fingers dramatically.

Sadie eyed him warily. "And you'll just talk to him for me?" Sadie knew she was many things: funny, sassy, occasionally bratty; but stupid, she was not.

Sure enough, the familiar grin slid across his face. She might not understand everything he said, but apparently, that leer was the same worldwide. "I will talk to him for you. If you do something for me in return."

Sadie looked from one captor to the other. The woman hadn't so much as made a sound during the course of the conversation. However, her gaze never left Sadie's face. The effect was extremely unnerving and Sadie felt herself squirming on the cot.

She looked back at the man. "You want to fuck me and I don't even know your name."

"Call me *Monsieur.*"

She gestured to his silent sidekick. "I guess she's *Madame?*"

"No, she's Therese."

"Does she ever speak?" Sadie looked at the immobile Therese. "Or move?"

He chuckled. "She will when the time is right. Now, do we have a deal?"

She looked him over. "What if I want to stop?"

"You may stop anytime you want."

Sadie took a deep breath. "Fine. I agree."

If Sadie was going to be perfectly honest with herself, she'd admit that she'd been ready to say yes when she first realized what he was going to ask. She wasn't horny, and he wasn't particularly good looking. It was something else, something primal about him. She'd seen it glint in his eyes. Besides, she was curious how the mysterious Therese fit into the picture.

Monsieur's eyes crinkled as he smiled. *"Bon. Therese, la porte."*

The woman stood up and unlocked the door of the cell. *Monsieur* said something to her in rapid French that Sadie didn't catch. Therese stood next to her and gestured for her to stand.

Sadie stood and Therese started pulling at her clothes. At the woman's wordless direction, Sadie slipped off her shoes and pulled off her socks. She winced as her feet hit the grimy floor, praying that it had been cleaned sometime recently. Therese removed Sadie's shirt and jeans. Sadie assumed that *Monsieur* was giving her orders. He spoke; Therese acted and then waited for him to speak again.

Therese then turned Sadie around and bent her over the cot. Sadie balanced herself on her elbows as the other woman gently pushed her legs apart. Monsieur barked another command, and Therese took up her post in the corner.

Sadie stayed still, waiting for something to happen. Her nerves stood on end, and she hung her head, trying to keep herself together. A moment later, she felt a touch so light, she thought she had imagined it. The pressure came a little harder the second time, and this time spread over her butt and the backs of her legs. The motion pulled against her panties, rubbing against her clit. She tried to arch herself against the fabric, but the hands stopped and held her still.

He placed a finger on her pussy, then slid it inside her. "Wet already? Therese, I think our little American slut is ready."

Therese nodded, but Sadie was sure the woman hadn't understood him. *Monsieur* pulled her panties down and continued to finger-fuck her until her legs started to sag. He withdrew from her, and she waited eagerly, sure his dick would follow.

Instead, his hand collided loudly with her cheeks. Sadie jumped, ass smarting.

"What the hell! You wanted to fuck."

He didn't say anything, but just rubbed his target until the stinging subsided. Sadie instinctively looked at Therese, but the woman's eyes were fixed on Sadie's butt. To Sadie's surprise, her mouth was slightly parted and her hands were clutched together. Sadie willed herself to relax.

SMACK!

He spanked her again, then again on the other cheek. "Do you like that?" he murmured.

SMACK!

"Therese likes to watch." *SMACK.* "And I like the way your derriere moves when I hit it."

SMACK. SMACK. SMACK.

Sadie braced herself for the next one, but it didn't come. Another peek at Therese told her the woman was waiting as well.

Monsieur laughed deep in his throat. "You never know when it's coming. I might want to caress it," he rubbed his hands gently over her ass, running his nails over the skin. Sadie's hips bucked, the almost ticklish sensation driving her closer to the edge.

"But then, other times, I like it rough."

SMACK!

He smacked her again, affectionately this time. He rubbed her legs briskly, then called Therese. He pulled Sadie up and Therese sat on the bed in front of her. *Monsieur* eased Sadie back down over her lap. Therese's hands eased their way into Sadie's hair, her breasts pressing gently against Sadie's head.

"*Un.*"

Sadie was so shocked to hear the woman speak, the slap took her by surprise. Therese's fingers tugged her hair excitedly.

"*Deux.*"

"*Trois.*"

The smacks came in quick succession, the vibrations spiraling deep within her already sensitive ass.

"*Quatre.*"

Sadie moaned, waiting for the next slap.

Therese didn't disappoint her. "*Cinq.*"

She groaned, surprised to notice how turned on she was. She wrapped her arms around Therese, gripping her waist.

"Five more, Ms. Miller."

The next three came quickly, each harder than the last. Then Therese stopped counting. Sadie plowed her head into the woman's stomach, trying to force the next command from her. But she remained silent and *Monsieur's* hand drew lazy circles across her flesh.

Sadie dug her nails into Therese's back. The woman gasped. *"Neuf."*

SMACK!

"Dix."

Sadie steeled herself as *Monsieur* spanked her a final time. She cried out, pressing her face deeper into Therese's lap.

"Ms. Miller? It is done." *Monsieur* pulled her up, holding her steady. Sadie opened her eyes, to find Therese watching her. Unlike before, she offered a small smile. Sadie returned it, while waiting for her lower half to regain feeling.

True to his word, *Monsieur* spoke with her accuser and Sadie was released two hours later.

The next morning, Sadie passed the merchant who had accused her of stealing his wares. As she fingered a silver bracelet on his table, she wondered what a second offense would cost her.

PLEASANT SURPRISE

Maria Grigoriadis

1

Sometimes I think I am the luckiest woman in the world. Especially when I'm least expecting it. One night I was in my apartment watching TV all alone, minding my own business, when the doorbell rang. I answered it to find this cute woman I'd never seen before standing there.

"Hi," she said. "Are you ready?"

"Umm sure, I guess, for what?"

"Oh, you're funny tonight, aren't you?"

I was so confused. I didn't mean to be funny. I didn't even know what the hell was going on.

"Are you going to let me stand out here in the hallway, or are you going to invite me in?"

I didn't want to be rude, so I invited her in. When I said before she was cute, I wasn't kidding. She had a great little body that was evident even through the clothes she was wearing. Her jeans fit her so well I'd have been jealous of her, if her ass hadn't looked so appealing in them. She had on a tight T-shirt that showed off muscles she had obviously worked really hard to achieve. By the time I closed the door behind her and turned around to ask her who she was and what she was doing there, she had taken off her shirt. She wasn't wearing a bra. She didn't need one, really. Her breasts were small, but oh god were they beautiful. And apparently, it was colder in my apartment than I thought it was. Without her shirt on, it was delightfully obvious that her well-muscled arms were not the only part of her body that she had worked to perfection. Staring at her, I realized I just wanted to lick her abs. She was tan, though not overly so, and she had no tan lines. *Nice touch,* I thought. Before I could open my mouth to ask her all the questions I had for her, she rushed over to me, put her index finger to my mouth and shushed me.

"No talking, remember?"

Actually no, I don't remember, I thought. But, now I was *really* hoping that she would refresh my memory. She took my hand and led me around my apartment, until she found what she was looking for. When we got into the bathroom, she turned on the light and ran the water for the shower. Then she took off her jeans. No underwear. I was really beginning to like my newly found friend. She placed both of my hands on her breasts and then leaned in and kissed me on the mouth. Her tongue explored my mouth, while my hands did the same to her breasts. I tried once again to speak, but she bit my lower lip.

"I thought I said no talking."

This time her tone was stern, with a hint of annoyance. I could see that she had blood on her lips from where she'd bitten mine. This was getting serious, but my curiosity got the better of me, and I put my arms around her and began kissing her neck. This seemed to relax her and make her happy. She put her hands between our bodies, pushed me back a little bit, and began unbuttoning my jeans. She slid my pants and underwear to the floor together. I stepped out of my clothes. I reached for the buttons on my shirt, but she grabbed my hand and shook her head no. She unbuttoned my shirt for me and I could see surprise in her eyes when she saw I was not wearing a bra tonight either. She put her mouth on my breast and began rolling her tongue around my nipple. I ran my hands through her hair as she made my nipple hard in her mouth. She did the same to my other breast and I could feel the wetness between my legs. A moan escaped my mouth. She looked up at me, smiled, and guided us into the shower.

I don't think I've ever enjoyed a shower more in my entire life. Having her hands all over me as she shampooed my hair and washed my body was amazing. Her hands were so gentle as they made their way around my body. Although the water was steaming hot, I was shivering from pleasure and anticipation of what was to come. She would stop every few minutes to kiss me and occasionally wink at me and smile. I couldn't help but laugh. Who was this woman? And how had I ended up naked with her in my shower? I had so many questions for her, but I didn't want her to stop if I spoke, so I made better use of my mouth. I returned all of her kisses with a passion that surprised me, given that she was a stranger. I made my way around her body and kissed the back of her neck and her back as I reached around and held her breasts in my hands.

2
This time I was the one who led her around my apartment. When we got to my bedroom, I motioned for her to lie down on my bed. At first I just looked at her. Lying there. Beautiful. Naked. Waiting for me. Waiting to be touched, kissed. Waiting for me to put

my hands on her, in her. I got into bed next to her and propped myself up on my elbow. I continued to stare at her as I ran my fingers gently down her body, from her mouth, to her neck, between her breasts, down her belly to the hair between her legs. I lingered here as I twirled the hair between my fingers and watched her close her eyes and tilt her head back a bit. I rolled on top of her and used my eager mouth to travel the same path as my hand had just taken. With one breast in my mouth, teasing her nipple with my tongue, I squeezed the other nipple between my thumb and index finger. She sat up quickly and gave me a hurt look.

"Oww," she cried out. "That hurt."

"No, no. No talking. Relax. Lie back down."

I met her stare for a moment. When she didn't do as I told her, I kissed her hard on the mouth and forced her back down with the weight of my body. *Good girl,* I thought, as she stopped resisting me and I felt her body relax under mine. *I don't know who you are, or why you came to my door, but now that you're here in my bedroom, it's my bed and my rules*, I thought. I positioned my legs between hers and spread them apart. Sliding my hand between her legs, I felt her wetness. I teased her by sliding my finger around her clit, putting only the one finger in her. She arched her hips up to meet my hand each time I entered her. I could feel the rhythm of a woman who had been fucked before and needed it again.

I gave her what she came for. I wrapped my free arm under her and around her waist and then I drove my index and middle fingers into her deeply. She cried out again, but not a word was spoken. I matched the rhythm of her hips. After all, this was her fuck. I was here for her pleasure. Her moans were intoxicating to me. Everything else melted away around us. All I could see was her. All I could hear was her pleasure. All I could smell was her. I continued fucking her, putting three fingers inside and using my thumb to rub her clit. Soon she tightened around my fingers and her clit was hard under my thumb. When she came I enjoyed it, but only for a moment. I pulled my fingers out of her and slid between her legs. I put my mouth on her clit, feeling her pulse and throb in my mouth. I licked her swollen clit gently and she shuddered as I did so.

"Stop, stop, stop...please," she said in a whisper I barely heard. "Come back up here to me."

I did as she asked and we both stared at the ceiling on our backs for a few minutes. Thinking we were done, I closed my eyes and relished the moment. When she rolled on top of me and got between my legs I was surprised again. She put her hands under my knees and pushed my legs up. She put her entire mouth on me and began licking my clit. It felt so good to have her hot, wet mouth on me. When I came, she did something I love to have done to me. I couldn't believe she was actually doing it to me without my having to ask for it. She put her fingers inside me and kept them inside me until I stopped throbbing on her hand.

3

When we were both staring up at the ceiling again, she finally spoke to me.

"Thank you for that. You are everything you said you'd be. You didn't lie about yourself."

"Hold on, I've been dying to ask you all night, who *are* you?"

With that she sat upright and gave me a frightened look.

"What are you talking about? You don't know who I am? Aren't you Sue?"

"No, I'm not. My name is Alexis. How could you think I was someone else? Don't you know this Sue woman?"

"No, I don't know her. Well, that's not true. I know her. I

just have never seen her before. We met online last weekend. We exchanged some hot email, but we've never met. Last night she wrote that she wanted to meet. That's what tonight was all about. She told me to show up at her apartment wearing no underclothes, and take off my clothes immediately. And she demanded no talking, just sex."

I couldn't help myself; I began to laugh.

"You were not by any chance looking for Susan Davis, were you?"

"I don't know, there were no last names."

"5C?"

"No, 5D. Her email said 5D. I'm sure of it."

"Well, either she typed her apartment number in wrong, or you wrote it down wrong. Susan lives next door, and you and I have never exchanged email, hot or otherwise."

That was almost two years ago now. Susan still lives next door and every time Kate and I see her in the hallway, we wave extra hard to thank her for bringing us together. Then we rush into our apartment and have the hottest sex, just like I promised Kate we would have in the emails *we* eventually exchanged.

MOVING

Susan St. Aubin

Hey!" he calls to me every morning when I go by his house, where he sits on his front porch in a wooden rocking chair. His iron gray hair is clipped close to his head. *Retired military,* I think as I salute and walk on. He's lived just a block from me for years, but I've never met him. *Keep moving,* I tell myself. *Exercise is good for the heart.* But in spite of myself I feel warmth spreading between my thighs, a physical triumph over excess rationality. My heart needs more than exercise, and maybe he'll know enough to keep his mouth shut about the army.

Dream: I wake to the pine scent of freshly sawn wood in a house under construction. I crawl out of my sleeping bag on a bare pine subfloor and wander around, looking at the posts that mark where walls will stand, while wondering what sort of house this will be. I look through the skeletons of what might become bay windows at the oak trees outside. Sawdust coats the bottoms of my feet as I carefully step over loose nails that have fallen on the floor. Outside it's raining but the roof is already completed, so I'm safe and dry.

Every night I walk through this house, sometimes in bright sunshine, sometimes in moonlight, sometimes when it's so dark I can't see a thing and have only the wood scent to tell me where I am. Occasionally the house is finished, either in Victorian style with porches and gingerbread trim, or in smooth modern stucco, but the next time I dream, it has reverted to its wooden frame. Once I lifted a trapdoor to find a basement too dark to explore, and another time I looked up to see the beams of unreachable rooms upstairs. I never notice any workers in this house that seems to be constantly constructing and deconstructing itself.

Reality: I wake up in a modern house designed by my former husband, a partner in the architectural firm where I managed the office for thirty years. I walk every day, too, but outside, exploring the neighborhood where I've lived half my life. I never set foot on these sidewalks until I retired, but I drove past them on my way to and from the office where my actual life took place; where I met my husband, had baby showers for my two children, and had an affair with a young intern. I told my husband I was leaving him in the lunchroom, and divorced him with the help of the lawyer whose office was upstairs. The intern left the firm, and so did my husband. I stayed. There were other interns, other partners. Time passed. My sons grew up and left, my lovers disappeared. Now I can explore.

The houses in this neighborhood are all different, many designed by my ex-husband in the contemporary style of the one he built for us, with its roof that looks like a bird trying to escape the slate walls. There are still some older homes left, like the military man's, wood and shingle, surrounded by flowers and trees.

I'm drawn to his porch, but I'm so sure we won't like each other, I try to keep him out of my thoughts as I walk.

Since I was out of condition after all those years of driving, I began slowly, picking my way along the unfamiliar sidewalks. My feet were tender, so I saw an orthopedist, who prescribed shoes suitable for either walking or running.

"You should work up to a gentle jog," he told me. "Just enough to condition the muscles without jarring the bones of the foot. We want your feet to conform to a healthy position."

When I forced my nonconforming feet into the shoes, I was surprised to find they had a bounce to them that encouraged me to lift my legs and reenact the history of locomotion. Soon I was swinging my arms and hips 1940s style until, without my noticing when, my feet were leaving the ground in a 1970s jog, which hurt my knees so I slowed to the race-walking of the 1980s and '90s, lifting each foot high, crooked arms pumping. What happened to the 1950s and '60s? That was when people began driving everywhere. Before exercising for health became popular, someone walking or, god forbid, running, might warrant a call to the police for suspicious behavior.

People haven't walked as a means of transportation since I was a child watching from our second-floor apartment as they passed, men in suits and hats, women in high heels with purses dangling from their shoulders, everyone's arms swinging freely on his or her way forward to buses, stores, jobs, the future. I wonder if that man on his porch has these memories. Does he notice how people these days move to stay in shape (and in place) rather than to get somewhere?

"Hey!" he calls to me as I pass. "Where do you go in such a hurry every day?"

"Nowhere," I say. "I'm exercising. It's important to keep the joints moving."

"Why not take it slow then?" he asks. "It's too hot to rush."

It's a warm May morning, but not at all hot. The wisteria along his porch railing is starting to bloom, and I'm quite comfortable in my jeans and T-shirt. He takes a sip of what looks like iced tea but could be rum and coke or whiskey and soda for all I know. He points to his foot, which I notice is in a cast.

"Broke it running," he says. "No more marathons for me. I intend to relax and preserve what I have."

"Pickle himself, he means," I mutter as I jog away, then slow to a walk because my throbbing feet are having a nonconforming day and seem to want to go back to rest on his porch, a luxury I forbid them.

The next morning, so early there's still a bit of fog, he's already sitting in his rocker. I pass by swinging my arms, wearing a skirt with my walking shoes.

"Haven't you got there yet?" he calls.

"Nope," I answer, leaning against his picket fence.

"If you're not going anywhere, why not join me?" He lifts his glass.

What have I got to lose? The great thing about age is, once you hit sixty, you can only win. There's not much future to worry you, and the past is done.

"You've arrived," he says as I climb the steps to his porch, where I sit in a creaking wicker chair while he hobbles into the kitchen on his short walking cast to get me a glass of whatever it is he's drinking, which turns out to be iced tea with honey and lemon. The fog is lifting. Anything is possible.

He introduces himself as Bob, a name ordinary enough to be fake. I tell him to call me Linda.

Two men our age jog by with weights tied to their ankles.

"That builds muscle," I tell him. "I'm thinking of getting some."

"The harder you make it, the harder you'll try," he remarks.

Since I don't understand what he means, I nod and sip my tea. The ice rattles in our glasses as two older women race-walk by, their muscular legs moving in rhythm as if they're dancing to the same music.

He whistles low, but they pretend not to hear.

"My, my," he murmurs. "They say sex is the best exercise there is. They must be compensating."

"How would you know?" I snap. "They could be on their way to their lovers. They could *be* lovers. Anyway, they've left us in the dust." I watch them continue down the road, kicking their heels high to their private music.

"Relax," he says, his hand on the back of my head, fingers twining my short salt-and-pepper curls.

I feel a trail of sweat start down my back, which could be a hot flash though I'm past that, or could mean the day is warming up. I let his hand continue massaging my head.

"Congratulations on not coloring your hair," he says. "I hate those bottle colors, all the same. I like real hair, where each strand is different." He pulls out a red hair, a white one, a black one.

"Ouch! Stop that." I clap a hand to the back of my head, pushing him away.

He holds my hairs to the light. "Beautiful," he whispers as he blows them off his fingers, watching them float to catch on the bark of the maple tree next to the porch.

The next day is hot, so he invites me inside where it's dark and cool, the sunlight filtered through gauzy curtains.

"I should take those down," he says. "My wife always liked every window covered, but since she left I feel like opening things up."

I wonder what he means by left. Moved on to her eternal reward, or left for New York? Away for a month, or for good? He gives me a tour of the house, built in 1910, the oldest in the area. Three bedrooms upstairs, one with a queen-sized bed, two with single beds. I'm afraid he's going to lead me into the marriage bed, but instead we settle on a leather couch downstairs in his study, glasses of tea in hand.

"I don't know what I'm doing with all this space," he says. "I keep thinking someone in the family will need a place to stay, but that's not likely anymore. The kids have their own lives, their own homes. It's time to move."

With or without the wife? He leaves it open.

His tea-tasting mouth finds mine and we lock tongues while carefully setting our glasses down on matching end tables. I let him pull my T-shirt over my head, unhook my bra, take off my shorts. Protests are for kids; *no* is what you say to children. I unzip his pants. At our age it's *yes* all the way, my hand on his cock, his tongue on my clit, his saliva lubricating both of us. We are more limber than I'd imagined, juices flowing everywhere, even in our joints.

"See how easy it is when you stop trying so hard?" he whispers in my ear. He gets up and opens his desk drawer, pulling out a package of condoms in all colors. I gently finger them: red, yellow, blue, black. I choose green, for spring. My legs dodge his cast, but can't escape a small bruise or two as he climbs on top of me, his green shaft pumping slowly inside me, sliding against the back of my clit until I open and come. Then he, like a gentleman, follows.

I'm polite enough not to ask him what drugs he takes.

My visits with Bob become part of my exercise routine, but instead of beginning on his block, I go the other direction so I'll end up there in the early afternoon. He likes to lick the salty sweat from the small of my back, and nuzzle my damp armpits, saying he enjoys the scent of work he doesn't do. If my walking and running can be considered work, the results are obvious: my legs and hips are growing trim and muscular, and my feet no longer get sore. He's in good shape for a porch-sitter, with a firm stomach and muscular arms. When he gets his cast off, he shows me his secret: a book of Air Force exercises he's done for years, though he was never in the military.

"Too nearsighted," he explains. "I'm wearing contacts now so you wouldn't guess that without my glasses I couldn't find my way out of my dreams in the morning. Not to mention I can't stand the idea of the government telling me what to think."

He reveals the secrets of isometric exercise, which he says is the only good thing the Air Force ever came up with.

"You move each muscle individually. I could even do this when I had my cast on, but now that it's off, I can do so much more."

He tells me to extend my leg, showing me how to tense and release each muscle group while he licks his way from my toes to my cleft, then positions himself over me with his powerful arms, lowering and raising his body with his cock inside me, unusually hard this afternoon, which I sometimes don't like now that my cunt is as delicate as fine silk, but he squirts in Astroglide until I'm swimming along with him.

"Push-ups and sit-ups," he commands. "Raise your hips."

While he pushes down, I pull myself up with my stomach muscles; when he pulls up, I push down; in and out we go on, tantalizing each other, neither of us in any hurry to finish this jazzy ballet.

"What did you do in your former life?" I breathe as I pull myself up.

"Teach," he answers, pushing into me. "Middle school, high school. History. Geography. You?"

"Office manager. For an architect. Whom I married. Two boys. Then divorce."

His breath goes out suddenly in what could be interpreted as a laugh.

"We aren't there anymore," he says. "Move on. Pump me any way you want."

I could pump him for information about his wife and kids, but I decide to stick to the physical as I guide him onto his back and move up and down on him until I'm at an edge I can't seem to slide off. I roll him on top of me and whisper, "Push down, deeper," and then I hold his hips between my thighs until my pulsing cunt sucks him dry.

"You're relentless," he says, tucking my damp hair behind my ears, but he's the one who's still hard.

We trade medical notes: he sometimes takes Viagra in the afternoon. Mornings he can do without. I tell him about the hormone cream I've started using in my cunt to bring back its raw silk texture.

"Watch it, Linda," he warns. "That stuff can cause cancer."

"Life causes cancer," I say. "And it's not like I'm eating it. Does anyone really know the side effects of your drug?"

We laugh at our mutual danger, which is, after all, what makes it worthwhile to carry on, which we proceed to do.

Sometimes we test each other's memory.

"Do you have trouble remembering the names of people you've met?" he asks.

"Only if they're not important," I respond without thinking.

"And as for the people I've never met: who cares?"

"See how easy life can be if you relax?" he says, licking his thumb and pressing it to my forehead. "Forgetting is a critical comment. I'd give you a gold star if I could remember where I put them."

Now I run my whole route to Bob's place, arriving breathless and sweaty, stretching my strong legs on his front steps while he watches at the screen door. One day I notice the windows are bare and clean, stripped of their floaty curtains. When I go inside, I see that most of the living room furniture is gone, except for two armchairs.

"Come on upstairs," he says. "I'll show you what I've been doing."

The three bedrooms are empty, with drop cloths covering the floors.

"The Salvation Army came for the old furniture early this morning," he says. "Next, I'll paint, then maybe rent out the rooms. No one's coming home." He winks at me. "Want a room?"

"I have a house," I remind him. "I don't know if I want to give it up." But I've never liked that house, and what has all this walking and running been for if not to leave it behind?

"Then visit." He puts his nose to my head and inhales the scent of my hair. "Stay the night sometimes," he whispers in my ear. "The couch in my study folds out, or we could get a new bed for one of these rooms. Life can be easy if you don't try to hold on to the past."

"It could be," I say, leaving it open. My hand toys with the hem of his shorts.

In my dream, the walls of the house are forming. This time there's steady progress: Sheetrock one night, plaster the next.

The rough floors are covered with smooth cherrywood planks. I wander through, touching the door frames, painted and ready for doors. One night glass appears in the curved bay windows. There's a front porch, too, with a white wicker couch on it. It's an old fashioned gabled house made new, a house I know I'll find if I haven't already. It's time to move to another life.

OUT OF THE SHOWER

Maria Matthews

Out of the shower...into my bedroom...wrapped haphazardly in a towel and still dripping slightly from the bath...I find him waiting for me behind the door. As I walk into the room I feel him, smell him, sense him before I see him—strong and male and musky, determined. "Hi," he says, deftly flipping the towel from around my midsection. I make a perfunctory objection, but he laughs gently, knowing that he already has the upper hand. His hands find my shoulders and he guides me further into the room, closing the door. "Have any plans for the evening?" he inquires. "Apparently I have a date!" I chuckle.

The blindfold covers my eyes, and he guides me down onto the bed. The closet opens, then closes, and the rope arrives at my wrists. I half protest, not really wanting him to stop. It's part of the game. "Something different tonight, my dear," he intones in a faux–French waiter accent, his smile coming through in his words. "What's that?" I say, taking the bait. I'm still damp from the shower and the breeze from the ceiling fan cools my skin, making my nipples harden and my hair stand on end. "Detailed descriptions of every thing I'm going to do to you," he says deliciously. Usually, he's very quiet, but I love hearing him when we fuck. There's something outrageously intimate about hearing a man make noise during sex. I'm intrigued—I nod quietly and lie back.

"I'm taking my shirt off." He states this matter-of-factly, and I wonder if this will have the desired erotic appeal. It's so blunt. As he enumerates each article of clothing, my mind starts to wander, and the image in my head is filled with detail and interest. "My pants are on the floor" brings with it an image of an erect cock, ready for me, straining to release itself from the everyday underwear that I know he's wearing. The combination of the erotic and the mundane is enough to make me think that maybe he's on to something.

He comes over to the bed and kisses me softly, his tongue exploring my mouth for a moment, his hard cock brushing against me. "I need to go get some things from the dresser." I hear his footsteps cross the room, a drawer opening, and then the trip back to the bedside. I'm waiting, slightly wet and expectant, curled in on myself to retain a little heat. "I went shopping today, and I got some things that I think you'll like. I'm going to suck your nipples, then pinch them until they're nice and hard, and then put these clamps on them." I'm not given a chance to comment before his mouth latches on to my right tit, sucking insistently and not at all gently. I squeal in half pain, half pleasure and feel my cunt start to swell. As promised, his fingers follow, taking the nipple deliberately between thumb and forefinger and pinching hard enough to make me cry out. "Mmm...perfect— just hard enough." I hear him rummaging around—removing something from a package?—then returning in earnest to his task. I feel cold metal on my nipple, but no real pressure. He releases the clamp, and it falls coldly against my breast. He picks it up, adjusts the screw, and reapplies it. This time, the pinch is intense—cold and hard and unrelenting. I cry out and squirm, but he holds me down. "Hey, I told you what I was doing! If I don't clamp them tight, they won't be tender when I take the clips off." I concede and, knowing that whatever he has planned for later is probably a sensualist's dream, I elect to wait it out as he gives the other nipple the same treatment. As the clamp bites down, I jump, but save the squeal for later.

When both tits are clamped, I hear him rummaging again. A few minutes go by with no contact and no words, and I start to wonder what he could be doing. Just then, he speaks up. "I'm putting a large, clear dildo into your hole. I want to watch your wet pussy swallow it up." My legs are pushed apart and the head of the implement rubbed insistently between my lips. "I'm going to push apart your lips with my fingers so that I can see everything." I hear him smiling again. "Wow, you're really, really wet." He separates my lips with his fingers, and my clit rises to meet him. He toys with the swelling bud, and then rams the rod into me several times. No niceties, no frills, just unrepentant fucking. My hips buck up, rising to meet him. "No, I'm not fucking you yet. This is just a placeholder. Your pussy is going to be starving for me when I get there." I feel him place a harness over the dildo and around my legs to keep me from expelling it, and resign myself to the sensation of my muscles working around the fake cock that I am stuck with.

"I'm going to pull the clamps off your tits now." Before I get a chance to protest, he pulls the clamps unceremoniously and they snap off with a satisfying sound. I hear them hit the ground as he pinches my left nipple, then the right. "I know this hurts, and I know you like it. I think you want me to play rough." I moan in response, dizzy with the sensations. "I'm going to hold your nipple steady while I play with it. I want to lick it, pinch it, bite it…and you're not going to move while I do it. If you do, I'll tie your legs and waist down, too." I can just see the leering grin on his face while I try desperately not to move. "Stick your tits out—I don't want you cowering away from me as if you don't like this. I know you do. I see the juice dripping from your cunt, out around the dildo." I jut my chest forward and feel his fingers gently pinching the soft flesh of my areola to make the rock-hard nipple stand out.

I feel his teeth on my sore nubs. The clamps have sensitized things a good deal, and I squeal and squirm. He nips, sucks, and every so often, bites. He is groaning his pleasure, and I feel his dick brushing my inner thigh. I gasp and try to stay still. After giving very thorough attention to the left side, he moves to the right. I feel his hands on both breasts and enjoy the feeling. Then he pinches both nipples at once, hard, rolling them between his fingers and finishing with a pointed treatment with fingernails from both hands. I scream and pull back, and my pussy swells and drips.

"Okay, I'm going to get more rope." He walks away and I know I'm in for a thorough fucking. This kind of thing gets us both off. He comes back and binds me, giving me the blow by blow report. "I'm tying your legs to the bedposts so that you can't wiggle out of my reach. Now, I'm adding some restraint around your waist so that you can't move those delicious tits out of my hands. I'm pulling the cock from your box so that you'll be hungry for me." I feel the dildo leave, and the walls of my pussy flare up, a torrent of fluid following the latex head out of the tunnel.

"Now, I'm going to surprise you. You obviously wanted more since you moved after I told you not to." I feel his mouth, his hands on me again. His fingers surround my areola, pointing the nipple skyward. There's a pinching feeling, then again and again, and then a lightning bolt from the nipple down to my clit.

My right nipple burns, the pinch almost unbearable. I feel him guide the left nipple up, licking it and biting it until it stands straight. Then the pinching again, but less time until the lightning bolt this time. His cock meets my lips. "Suck my dick," he says, without ceremony, grabbing a handful of hair and guiding my open mouth to his rod. I lick, suck, taste and savor, all the while feeling my nipples sending insistent messages downward.

He pulls from my mouth, quickly and without warning. The rope binding my waist and ankles is swiftly cut and removed, and I feel his swollen head glide into my throbbing pussy. He pounds me, over and over again, my feet on his shoulders and my ass bouncing off the bed. He pulls the blindfold off my eyes. "I want to look at you while we fuck." I blink at the light, and look him straight in the eye as every wave of pleasure ripples through my body. He pulls what turn out to be clothespins off my nipples, takes one in his mouth and the other in his fingers, and comes. I scream my approval and shudder at the sensation of him shooting off into me.

He loosens the remaining restraints, freeing my wrists. As if suddenly recalling his promise to articulate his actions, he grins at me. "I want you to rub my cum over your clit until you come," he says, sitting up but staying firmly lodged in me. I reach down and slide my fingers around, feeling the dripping cum and pulling it upward toward the swollen bud. I rub and caress, pinching and pulling at my clit until the waves of pleasure force his member back out into the cold world.

He falls on top of me and I welcome his familiar weight with satisfaction. Wrapping my arms around him and rolling over, I nuzzle into the crook of his neck, feeling content and very well pleasured. The room smells deliciously of sex and sweat, and I drift into sleep wrapped warmly in him.

LOVE TRIANGLE

B. J. Franklin

Would you like to live forever?"

I blinked. "Would I like to *what*?"

"Live forever. A scientist quoted in the paper said that, in twenty-five years' time, he'll be able to prevent aging. If he gets the funding."

"Sounds like a scam to con billionaires into giving him their money." Lindsay was a great friend, but when she got hold of an idea, she didn't want to let go.

"Wouldn't it be fun to see what changes over the next thousand years? Who knows, by then you might have found the courage to ask Simon out."

I rolled my eyes. "Very funny."

"Come on, Jeanie, admit it. You fancy him like crazy."

"Of course, he's gorgeous. But there are hundreds of girls running after him. Let's change the subject."

"Look, if he doesn't feel the same, he's an idiot, and we'll get drunk together. But you really need to move on."

I sighed. "I will never have the courage to ask him out."

"Then invite him to dinner and play footsie under the table. Tickle him until he promises to give you multiple orgasms all night. And if that doesn't work, you can always give him *my* phone number."

"Lindsay," I groaned. "He'd probably love your phone number. You're small and blonde with a perfect figure. I'm overweight with mouse brown hair and glasses. He'd laugh in my face."

I thought Lindsay was going to explode. "I've never heard anything so ridiculous in my life!" A hush fell as other people in the café turned to stare. "Who's been telling you such nonsense? If it was that ass George, I'll beat him up."

The thought of Lindsay, five feet nothing, beating up the six-feet-four mass of muscle that was my ex-boyfriend should have made me laugh, but her expression was so fierce I could see that George would've had no chance.

"It wasn't him," I lied. "Anyway, there are plenty of overweight men in the world, and one of them will suit me fine. I was just pointing out why I have zero chance with Simon."

"You were just nothing. If you're doing anything this Saturday, cancel it. We have a date."

"To do what, exactly?"

"To visit a little shop I know, so you can see how gorgeous you really are."

I opened my mouth to object, but she was already putting on her jacket. "You can pay for coffee, as Saturday is my treat. It can be your birthday present. I've been wondering what to get. I'll pick you up at ten."

"My birthday's in November and it's only August," I protested, but she'd already gone. What on earth was I going to do?

I begged, pleaded and promised, but to no avail. Saturday found us both inside a smart lingerie shop in the center of town. Lindsay dragged me past the open-mouthed assistant, past all the pretty matching sets and elegant teddies, straight to a small section at the back. I stared at the rack of vinyl and leather in front of me. "You have got to be kidding."

Lindsay, of course, wasn't listening. "These should do nicely," she said, thrusting a small pile into my arms and steering me into a changing room. "Don't put anything aside before you've shown me what it looks like on," she ordered as she yanked the curtain across.

I looked down at the pile.

There was a bright red contraption on the top, with straps and hooks everywhere. I put it aside for when I was feeling braver. Next came a bright blue corset-style top, with four suspender straps hanging from the bottom and hooks all the way down the back. After forcing the two sides together, I did up the first few hooks, which promptly terminated my ability to breathe.

"Lindsay…"

"Just put it on. It'll fit fine, I promise, once they're all done up."

Did she have X-ray vision or something? I hoped not, as with more straining and weird noises, I eventually succeeded. God only knows what the rest of the shop thought I was doing. There was a full-length gilt mirror down one wall, but I couldn't face it yet. I adjusted the straps so they weren't cutting into my shoulders and positioned the cups properly. It was then I realized that breathing was possible—in a tight but not unpleasant way. It had to be a good sign. I opened my eyes.

My squeal stunned the shop into silence. "I have a waist!"

The curtain was yanked back and Lindsay was there, running a professional eye over me. "See, told you."

I wouldn't have believed it if I hadn't seen it. The corset style held me in and made me look, not thin, but...shapely. My curves looked sleeker, smoother, tighter. I felt sexy.

I smiled.

"It's good, but not quite right. The color's wrong." Lindsay was unmoveable. Well, she was paying. A quick peek at the tag made me shudder. For that price, the damn hooks should have been platinum.

None of the other outfits were what she wanted, either. We were almost at the bottom of the pile and I was becoming an expert with the fiddly little clasps. "Last one," I called, as I pulled it off the hanger. It was a black top, but longer than the others. And it didn't have straps. I liked that. The extra inch or so of material meant it might almost cover my...Jesus. It wasn't a top at all. It was a dress.

In for a penny. It slipped over my head like silk. Most of it was solid material, except for an oval-shaped window at the back. After my usual Birdy-Song-cum-salsa-dance, I got the dress fastened and the material smoothed down. It fit like a glove—one that was a size too small. I turned to the mirror, and saw my face crease into a huge grin. This was the one.

The black vinyl, like the first one I'd tried, held me in and made my curves look mouthwatering. It clung to me, leaving nothing to the imagination, but still looked elegant. There were three small purple bows on it, two on the hem and one on the shoulder, and there were three narrow, vertical strips of purple stitching spaced around the front. The vertical bands made my legs look longer and my hips slimmer. I loved it. If I had to look like a hooker, at least it was a high-class one.

"Perfect," Lindsay sighed from the doorway. "Take it off, and I'll get them to pack it up for you."

She refused to let me pay anything toward it, and got in a

huff when I tried to buy a pair of lace hold-ups to match. "You have gorgeous skin," she insisted. "Show it off."

I did get a shock when I realized she didn't intend for me to wear any underwear at all. "The dress is way too short. He'll be able to see...well, everything!"

Lindsay remained calm. "Exactly. Start as you mean to go on."

I could always come back another time.

As we walked to the bus stop, I was convinced that everyone could see inside the bag, but we reached it before my paranoia got out of control. As Lindsay was giving me some parting words of advice, I felt a tap on my shoulder.

"Hi, Jeanie. Been shopping?"

It was him. Simon. His wavy dark hair fell invitingly over his forehead, and his deep blue eyes shone with innocent interest. A beetroot blush spread over my face, and I made a vague murmur of agreement, clutching the bag even tighter. If I dropped it and the dress spilled out, I would never survive the shame. A pack of girls across the street were gazing at him in admiration, but he was oblivious to their attention.

We chatted for a few minutes, but I have absolutely no memory of what we said. He smiled at me before he left, and my knees grew weak. Lindsay was right. I couldn't go on like this. It was getting ridiculous.

At half-past five that afternoon, I stood outside Simon's door, biting the fingernails on one hand and clenching his spare key tightly in the other. I was wearing the minidress, black high-heeled boots and an overcoat. No underwear.

It wasn't too late to change my mind. Once I was inside, it was do or die, but if I left now, no one would know. Except Lindsay, and she'd never shut up about it—but if I was going to go through with this, it would be for me. That way, if it all went pear-shaped, there'd be nobody to blame but myself. For a moment, I considered the humiliation I'd suffer if he really didn't fancy me. Still, I looked good, I felt good, and I would always regret it if I left now with my tail between my legs.

The decision was made. Lindsay would be proud.

I opened the door and replaced the spare key under the holly bush. The bedroom was the obvious place to wait. I'd been to his flat before, but had never seen inside that inner sanctuary.

The bed was massive. It dominated the room, and the thought of all the women Simon had probably had on top of it made me pause. But I wasn't backing down now.

I stretched out on the dark blue bedding and waited. And waited. Every second felt like an hour as anticipation began to build, sending shivers down my spine.

At quarter-to-seven, I heard a key turn in the lock. Finally. But there were two voices in the hall outside. If Simon had brought a girl back, I was going to dissolve into a puddle of embarrassment right there on the cream carpet. I strained my ears to catch what they were saying, but only indistinct murmurs filtered through.

Suddenly, there was silence except for creaking floorboards. I was concentrating so hard, it took me a few seconds to realize the creaking was getting nearer. They were coming toward the bedroom. *Shit!*

I made a dive for the en suite bathroom, only just reaching it in time. The bedroom door was flung open and passionate kissing noises were clearly audible. Forget the whole "no one to blame but myself" pep talk, I was going to kill Lindsay. This was all her fault.

I couldn't resist a quick peep. Did Simon prefer blondes or brunettes? I peered round the still partly open door and got the

shock of my life. Simon was wrapped around a tall, blond...
man. He was *gay*? Terrific. My humiliation was complete. All I
could do was pray to every deity I knew that somehow I could
escape unseen, and return to my uneventful, suddenly idyllic-
seeming life with Simon none the wiser. I'd just sit on the edge of
the bath and wait. In a minute or two.

I'd never seen two men kiss before.

The man with Simon was less classically good looking, but
a few inches taller, and as blond as Simon was dark. His black
trousers and white shirt outlined an equally muscular build. Lips
and tongues moved in perfect harmony, merging and separating
in an erotic dance, and their arms were wrapped tight around
each other. I'd fantasized about watching two men kiss, but to
see it for real... I wasn't surprised when my body responded. My
breasts became full and tight, and my nipples ached. Moisture
trickled between my legs as the hard peaks rubbed against the
silk, growing harder with each accidental touch. When I looked
down, I could see them straining against the material, like little
twin soldiers standing to attention. Oh, how badly I wanted to
touch them.

But my attention was diverted by what the men were doing.
Simon's head was thrown back, and pleasure was written all
over his face as the other man squeezed his nipples through the
shirt.

"Paul..." Simon moaned, and the man smiled.

"You're so turned on already. Did you see your hot little
friend today?" Paul's voice was deep, inviting and in total control. I was so seduced by it, at first I didn't realize what he was
saying.

Simon nodded. "She was out shopping."

"I thought so. Seeing her always has this effect on you." He
unbuttoned Simon's shirt and found his nipples again.

Simon shuddered and pressed closer to Paul. "She's so...cute. I can't help it."

I couldn't believe it. They were talking about me. I squeezed both my nipples desperately, and twin darts of pleasure shot straight to my groin. But it wasn't enough. I wanted Simon's large, calloused hands on my breasts, cupping and stroking. Paul's mouth on my stomach, edging lower...

Simon moaned, and I remembered where I was. A real-life fantasy was being acted out in front of me. My imaginings could wait.

Paul was speaking: "...told her about us yet? I know how much you want to confess the horny details." One finger was stroking up and down the bulge in Simon's jeans, and Simon's whole body was trembling.

"Please."

"Imagine it. She's so turned on. Her nipples are so tight and hard, and she's moaning so beautifully. You can't resist teasing them with your tongue, just for a moment. Yes, she likes that. Just a bit longer."

Paul's fingers were now inside the jeans, his hand wrapped around Simon's cock, and Simon's hips were bucking helplessly. He was nearing climax. I could tell from his face. I slipped a hand under my dress as Paul's hypnotic voice continued the fantasy.

"Her breasts are so plump and soft, even through the material. You need to see them, don't you? Quivering and eager, with hard, brown nipples. Such a naughty girl, not wearing a bra, but you're so excited, you don't care. You want your hands slick and wet, rubbing moisture all over those tits. You want to press them together so you can slide your cock in between them, trapping it in that slick passage as she squeezes her own nipples in excitement, watching you move back and forth, back and forth...."

My fingers were echoing his words, one hand on my breast and the other moving eagerly over my clit. I was close. And so was Simon.

Suddenly, Paul withdrew his hand and stepped back. Simon staggered for a moment, then recovered enough to glare at Paul. "What the hell are you doing?"

Paul met his gaze calmly, but I could see the bulge at his groin. "Punishing a bad boy for having such wicked thoughts about a close friend. She'd be horrified if she knew. I think...yes. A good spanking will do. Get undressed, but keep the briefs on."

Simon licked his lips. "A spanking?"

Paul sat down on the bed, his eyes doing the talking. Standing up is supposed to be a position of power, but all the control was in Paul's hands, and both men knew it. I never doubted what Simon would do.

He undid the last few buttons on his shirt, and the muscles in his shoulders and arms rippled invitingly as it dropped to the floor. Shoes and socks followed, and then he eased the jeans over his swollen cock and down strong, muscular thighs. The jeans joined the pile on the floor, and he looked at Paul.

Paul's arms fastened round Simon's waist as he placed him facedown across his lap.

"I feel stupid," Simon muttered, and I wanted to laugh. But only for a moment. Paul's hand came down sharply in response, and the slap was very loud in the silent room. Simon gasped.

"Again?" Paul asked, and Simon nodded.

The hand came down once more, and Paul started counting. "Two, three, four, five..." Simon was squirming, and each slap was punctuated by a sharp intake of breath. His erection was rubbing against Paul's groin, and watching their faces as their cocks rubbed together was driving me crazy.

I braced myself against the wall and my fingers found my clit.

The picture of the two men in the next room was imprinted on my mind, and their aroused grunts and moans could be clearly heard. I flicked my clit faster and faster. I was going to come. Then the noises had stopped. Had they climaxed already? Damn it, I wanted to come with them. I opened my eyes.

Paul was lounging in the bathroom doorway, watching me with a smile on his face. "Don't stop on my account," he urged. Then, as I just stared at him in mounting horror, he said, "Do you have a name?"

I swallowed. "Would you believe me if I said no?"

"Jeanie, is that you?" Simon exclaimed. "What are you doing here? Is everything all right?"

I closed my eyes, but opened them again when Paul chuckled. "So, you're Simon's hot little friend." He eyed my heaving breasts with masculine appreciation. "Hot, definitely," he murmured. "But little...certainly not."

My nerve broke. "Excuse me," I gasped, and ran for the door. I hoped to dash past before he could react, but he clasped my arms and swung me round to face him. His grip was firm, but his voice was gentle.

"You can't leave now, we're just getting to the good part. Simon will be so disappointed. Maybe I can persuade you to stay...."

His lips closed over mine, and my clit pulsed. They were warm and soft, coaxing me to respond, and his hands felt so strong. His tongue was slow and sure as it teased my lips, and they instinctively parted. His erection nudged my thigh and I wiggled eagerly, trying to get closer.

Another hard, male body was suddenly pressed against me from behind, and another pair of warm lips was trailing kisses down my neck. How did he know my neck was so sensitive? It felt divine, and I melted into their arms.

"Was this Lindsay's idea?" Simon whispered in my ear.

I nodded.

"I must remember to thank her."

Paul raised his head. "Indeed. But as stunning as you are in that outfit, it needs to come off." He dealt with the fastenings in seconds. Clearly, it wasn't his first time.

I stepped out of it, and nervously turned to face them.

"Beautiful," Paul breathed, and Simon's eyes echoed him silently. I blushed, aware I was grinning like an idiot, but unable to help it.

Paul gently removed my glasses and placed them on the windowsill. Then he put his hand on my stomach. "I'd love to explore these curves, but Simon's about to explode."

"I can last a bit longer," Simon said quietly, his eyes fixed on my jutting nipples.

"In that case..." Paul took my hand and led me to the bed, lying down on it and pulling me down next to him. "I'm going to play with your tits, and I'm sure Simon wants to join me."

I shuddered with delight as Simon joined us on the bed, one man on each side of me. Every caress, every look spoke of desire. I'd never felt so sexy, or so turned on. Simon's touch was softer than Paul's, less expert, but just as arousing. My nipples were stroked and teased, and the pleasure intensified when hands were replaced by mouths. Soft, warm lips suckled at each breast, and I got wetter and wetter. One dark head and one blond were framed against my fair skin, and the visual contrast was incredible. I couldn't tear my eyes away.

Paul kissed slowly down from my breast to my stomach, where he lingered until I was begging him to move lower. I tried to force his head where I wanted it, but he resisted, and then Simon caught my wrists and pinned them to the bed. I meant to tell him to let go, but I kept forgetting, and finally I realized I didn't want him to.

Paul kissed all the way down to my foot, and suckled each toe in turn before licking an unhurried path up the inside of my leg. The back of my knee was given special attention, and by the time he reached my thigh, I was desperate. The evil snake used his tongue carefully in the crease at the top, then switched to the other leg and began the whole process again. "Bastard," I hissed, and he dared to laugh.

Simon was enjoying my excitement. He let go of my wrists, pressed my breasts together, and took both nipples into his mouth at once. It felt great, and he'd somehow lost his briefs along the way so his erection was rubbing frantically against my thigh. That felt even better.

I stroked his hair with one hand and sent the other exploring. There were small male nipples that were deliciously sensitive, sleek muscles and soft, springy hair to discover. His penis was stiff and swollen, but velvety soft. I wanted more.

He was grunting and thrusting into my hand. I tugged his head away from my breasts and looked into his eyes. "Please," I whispered, and tried to guide him sideways. He moved quickly once he realized what I wanted. Soon he was flat on his back on the bed, angled slightly so I could reach his groin, his feet pointing past my head. Paul was just sucking on my little toe, and I took all my frustration out on Simon. Payback can be such a bitch.

Simon's eyes burned with lust as my fingers teased his inner thighs. I savored the warm satin and his erection strained toward me, but it would have to wait a bit longer. I rolled his balls tenderly in the palms of my hands, and he sighed with pleasure.

Paul's mouth, which had been edging toward my thigh, stopped. "What a great idea," I heard him say, but was too distracted to look. I leaned forward, wrapped a hand around Simon's cock, and took the head into my mouth. He tasted of sweet salt and male arousal, and smelled like Simon. His hips thrust faster and faster, and I felt him lift his head to watch. He was enjoying the show.

There was movement to the side of me near Simon—Paul's legs and lower body were wiggling about in my peripheral vision. Finally he relaxed on the bed. His cock was erect and straight, and the tip twitched as his hand idly caressed it. Simon's cock was swelling and throbbing in my mouth, and I knew he was watching Paul touch himself. Then Paul's tongue returned to my thigh, and my pussy flooded. Damn, I wanted to come. But Paul again refused to speed up—until, that is, Simon's mouth closed round his cock. That was what Paul's maneuvering had been for. His tongue slipped a little toward my muff, but resumed its teasing. Simon was clearly used to giving head, and from the look on his face, he loved it. I certainly loved watching him.

Paul's tongue was still tormenting the top of my thigh, and I'd had enough. Paul seemed quite prepared to stay there all night.

I started sucking Simon's cock in earnest, rhythmically stroking the shaft, and almost immediately it had the desired effect. Simon's increased arousal was passed on to Paul through the mouth clamped round his cock, and Paul faltered. I took his head in my hands and urged it toward my pussy.

He tried to resist, but I think the scent of my arousal drew him on, and after his first taste, he was hooked. His hands parted the soft folds and his tongue began to probe inside. I trembled as he flicked my clit over and over again. It was a delicious chain reaction, and I wanted it to last forever, but of course it couldn't. Pleasure was quivering along every nerve, and I was too close to the edge. Simon was thrusting faster and faster into my mouth, but my eyes were fixed on his tongue wrapped around Paul's cock, and the look on his face as he teased and coaxed Paul to climax.

Pressure built inside me with every flick of Simon's tongue I glimpsed, and with every corresponding suck Paul gave to my clit. Their grunts of arousal and their harsh breathing was the sweetest of music, and their excitement was irresistible. I came fast and hard, and the peak was so intense, I almost forgot where I was. But Simon still hadn't come, and his moans were getting desperate.

I ran my nails lightly down his perineum, that responsive area of skin between balls and anus, and squeezed his shaft with my other hand. He shouted my name as his seed spurted into my mouth, and I swallowed without thinking, claiming my prize. A few seconds later, Paul's cries joined ours, and I couldn't stop trembling as I watched Simon swallow as eagerly as I had.

When I recovered, my head was cushioned on Simon's thigh, and Paul's head was resting on mine. Simon's head was in a similar position on Paul's stomach.

Paul's stomach was flat and beautifully toned and gazing at it, I felt all my insecurities come flooding back, but I refused to let them ruin the moment. The men loved my curves, they'd made that clear, and besides, there had to be enough of me to go round. There were two of them.

My clit pulsed, and I smiled. Even the thought was exciting. A spark of light caught my eye, and I looked over to see the three of us reflected in the distant bathroom mirror, all curves and soft edges in the shadows. "How beautiful," I whispered. "A perfect triangle." Then I giggled. "A sex triangle."

Paul stirred and planted a gentle kiss on my stomach. "Not a sex triangle," he corrected sleepily. "A love triangle."

Simon murmured in agreement. My heart swelled as I looked at them, and I was still smiling when sleep claimed me, lured by the warm contentment that surrounded us.

Lindsay never lets me forget that it was all her idea. Simon and Paul treat her like a beloved younger sister—much to her pretended disgust. She knows they would never look at another woman except me, and what on earth would make me want to look at other men?

They will insist on giving me chocolates. They say I need the calories to replace the ones we burn up together. Once I suggested dieting, and they threatened to throw the diet sheets out the window. "One of the first places you'll lose it from is your breasts," Simon said fervently. "No way."

It's nice to be appreciated. Though if any of us does put on weight, we'll all have a hell of a time fitting on the bed, huge as it is. Lindsay joked we should replace all the furniture with a gigantic wall-to-wall bed that takes up the whole room.

Now there's a thought.

HET CATS

Jean Roberta

The call of the saxophone pulled me into the room. The notes were brazenly sly, with a vibrating undertone that slid under my midnight-blue halter top with the built-in bra and the clingy sarong skirt that was supposed to make me look like a Wild Woman from the Tropics, even though the outfit matched. I licked my crimson lips and pushed my wavy chestnut hair out of my eyes.

"Hey, girlfriend!" sang Barry in my ear, over the insinuations of the horn, the tinkle of the keyboard, the bump-and-grind of the drums. He pulled me close by sliding a hand around my furthest hip, taking his time. I knew without looking that the warm hand leaving invisible tracks on me was lightly-furred, bold-knuckled and neatly manicured. I shifted my weight, teasing him with my haunches. "Love the color, Lee," he teased back. "You're finally learning what goes with your skin." So bitchy, so Barry.

Spotting one of his favorite young men, he called, "Hey,

twink! Who's your daddy?" As the last note from the saxophone left me hanging, Barry moved away without a backward glance. As he casually showed me his back, I noticed the tight leather that encased his narrow male butt. *Did anyone besides bikers wear leather in the 1950s?* I made a note to myself to look it up. I touched my metal garters through the shamelessly synthetic fabric of my skirt; they were as authentic as I could find.

The band kicked into a high-energy rock song about a second chance at love. I needed a dance partner, someone to seduce in classic style at Fifties Nite in the queer bar.

Gail, my ex from several years ago, was standing at the bar in a Dick Tracy suit and fedora, her hand on the back of a woman in a full, polka-dot skirt and frizzy blonde hair. "Gail!" I announced, touching her shoulder. She turned, looked and grinned before she spoke; that was a good sign. I smiled at her companion, who looked uneasy.

The lead male singer and horn player was clutching a mike as though he wanted to make out with it. He looked like a Mike himself. "Bay-bees," he crooned, "all you hepcats and kitties in jiveland, we're gonna rock you one more time and then take a break and we'll be right back atcha. I'm your big daddy Eugene, and our lovely lady here is Joo-dy"—she smirked to a drumroll and a chorus of wolf whistles—"and our man on the skins is boppin' Bob"—*ba-dum!*—"and here's Len on gee-tar"—*twangg*—"and Reg on the keys." A pair of hands rolled smoothly over the keyboard from low to high. "We all drink Molson because We Are Canadian."

"Wooo!" answered the audience closest to the stage. I recognized Barry's baritone.

He never needed a mike, and I couldn't lose track of him as long as he was making noise. I knew he liked to sing, and I wondered if I could ever get him to do it just for me.

"Dance with me, Lee, you hussy," chuckled Gail, reaching for me as she patted her date reassuringly. We moved to the dance floor in synch, like old friends, even as I remembered why I had broken up with her: her double-bind games. She had a way of showing me off, then blaming me for attracting too much attention, especially from the wrong people. I wasn't planning to stop now.

Gail could jive as though she had lived through be-bop first-hand. She twirled me and swung me, and I welcomed the distraction. I could still keep up with her.

Barry was dancing beside me with his twink of the moment, watching me. He was swiveling his hips and moving his shoulders, showing me his moves as though I cared. The boy followed Barry's eyes, then gave me the patronizing smile of a senior to a freshman. Obviously he thought I was no threat: only a chick.

I had been good at skipping rope as a child, and I willed myself back into that rhythm and speed. Moving with the beat, I leaned in close to Barry's face. "Why are you such a slut in public?" I stage-whispered, exaggerating the words so he could sight-read if his hearing had already begun to fail. His eyes and mouth both widened in mock surprise. I turned my attention back to Gail.

The song ended with a thump and whine from the guitar. "Thanks, babe," she cooed. She rested a hand possessively on my shoulder, under my hair.

"Ooo-ee, hot mamas and daddy-o's, there's some fine dancing goin' on this evening. We're gonna give you more of what you like and we're gonna slow it right down before the break, so grab the one you love best and hold on tight. This is a spot dance, so just keep movin' and wait for the light to shine on you. There'll be a prize for the best couple." Colored spotlights played wildly over the dance floor.

Gail's date was pushing her way through the crowd like a

tugboat through a choppy sea. A roving spotlight turned her face bright green, making her look like a sinister clown. She approached Gail with eyes like searchlights. I stepped aside, smiling graciously.

"You owe me a dance, Lee," joked Barry, wrapping his arms around me from behind, filling my nose with the manly smell of his cologne. "I need an old lady to keep me on the straight and narrow."

I snorted. "You didn't answer my question," I responded *sotto voce*. I didn't pull away.

Barry's twink was nowhere in sight. I assumed he must be in the john, or servicing a john, or perhaps both. I wondered whether too much contact with queens had coarsened my soul. Yet Barry always seemed like a different person outside the bar, especially on the home turf of his hair salon. I had always gone to him to have my hair cut, before I decided to grow it. I missed feeling his hands on my tingling scalp and hearing his low-keyed, philosophical take on the world's problems.

The notes of the saxophone cut through the air, wrapping themselves around us. Barry held me with the solemn gentleness of a teenage boy who thinks his date is breakable. We drifted around the floor, steering past other couples. Unbelievably, Barry pulled me closer. He pressed me against the rock-hard evidence of his admiration. I could feel wetness springing out of my temples, my armpits, my crotch. I needed an explanation.

"What the hell are you doing?" I hissed.

Barry pulled just far enough away to look into my eyes, one eyebrow raised. "Ummm," he hummed in time to the music. His body was firm, hot, as sheltering as a tree. "Oh, bay-bee, I've been waiting so long." He paused. "Don't tell me you don't want me, girlfriend."

It had never occurred to me that I might have to fight off

serious advances from him. I suddenly saw him as Man the Snake, a predator who had burrowed under my womanly defenses by posing as a friend. Odd, though, that I felt myself melting like the Wicked Witch of the West. "You're drunk," I pointed out. I wasn't sure if I was accusing him or convincing myself that none of this would count in the morning.

His hard smooth leather pushed maddeningly into my damp skirt. I could feel the heat of his chest even through the armor over my tits. "Drunk as a skunk, babe," he confessed sadly. "Fuel for the trip. You are one scary dyke."

I couldn't help snickering, especially since eyes were following us all over the dance floor. In this place, the sight of a man and a woman wrapped around each other held a kinkiness all its own. I had to laugh, or die of embarrassment.

"Aww-right! We got us a winning couple here this evening, a pair of smooth dudes with some cool moves. What are your names? Wayne and Kevin! Well, Wayne and Kevin, you've won yourselves a bottle of champagne and a romantic brunch for two at Chez Pierre!"

I wondered if Barry envied the winning couple. I was just relieved that the spotlight hadn't stayed on us for too long; the mere sight of us together could cause a short in the system.

The music was over, but Barry held me with the strength of perversity. How long had he been planning this campaign? Or had he been seduced by the retro spirit of the evening? That might be the same demon that prompted me to speak. "We could go for brunch too, lover," I purred. "I could wear a hat. You don't have to be scared, man. I only bite when I'm in heat."

Barry reached down and pinched my ass, hard. "Come on," he muttered, pushing me to the edge of the dance floor. I had forgotten how pushy men could be.

While the band was drinking their Molsons, the crowd seemed

as confused as a herd of cattle with no leader. Barry steered me single-mindedly through knots of our retro-chic acquaintances, ignoring the glances that followed us like sparks from cigarettes; small but potentially dangerous.

I saw his destination. Shock and disbelief flooded through me. "That's the women's can!" I whispered, trying without hope to be discreet. "If you think you're going in there, man, you don't know bar dykes."

I knew I had to prevent Barry from provoking a riot among the women, but I already felt like a traitor to my tribe. I wanted to be alone with him, just once. Friendship seemed like an amazing aphrodisiac.

To my great relief, he stopped and turned me to face him. "I know you've got stalls in there, Lee. And I know what else they're used for besides the usual. Can't you just think of me as a big bar dyke who wants you so much she can't wait?"

"Do you see me as one of your twinks?" I countered.

"Touché, girl," he laughed softly. "You like breaking the rules. Don't you want to sneak me in where the ladies powder their noses?"

"Jesus, Barry," I muttered, "I'm not sure you could fit into a stall with me. Aren't you parked outside?"

"You want my car? You wanna give it up on the backseat with songs from the Hit Parade on the radio? Anything you want, honey," he grinned.

"Let's go," I urged him. "I don't think we're welcome. Can't you hear the talk? 'Damn hets, why can't they stay in their own bars?' "

Bubbling with laughter to protect each other from the chill in the ambience, we went out the back door. The chill of the evening air was much more refreshing. Barry's familiar hand on my butt caused shivers of pleasure to run continuously up my spine as we crunched over the gravel of the parking lot to his venerable Oldsmobile. "Madame," he addressed me, holding the door open. "Let me take you for a drive."

The old boat of a car could skim over the mean streets of our town like a flying carpet. The actual streets were rough with cracks and potholes, caused by the harsh climate of the Canadian prairies and the limited repair budget of the local government.

As far as I knew, serious crime mostly existed in other places. I could pretend, though, that Barry was a bad boy of teenage fantasy, the one from the wrong side of the tracks who was taking me away from the well-paved, suburban expectations of my parents. As though reading my mind, he asked, "Mind if I smoke?"

"Yes," I told him. "But it does go with the outfit. Just be careful you don't burn your pants," I laughed.

He rolled his window down all the way before lighting a cigarette and resting his left elbow dangerously on the sill, leaving a shower of sparks behind us as he drove with one hand. The rebel-with-a-cause effect was convincing, and morally satisfying. It seemed only fair to me that Barry should be able to impersonate the hoods who used to beat him up in high school. Just as I, the nerd with the perpetual pile of books, had a right to play Prom Queen for a night.

We reached and passed the edge of town, where the prairie stretched on and on, apparently to infinity. The chirp of crickets, and the almost inaudible buzz of other living things, sounded like the breathing of Mother Earth. Barry pulled us off the road, and brought the car smoothly to a stop.

"Come here, girl," he ordered, and I nestled in his arms. As his hot lips pressed against mine, I could feel the roughness of a face that needed to be shaved every morning. His tongue coaxed my teeth to spread apart, mimicking another organ in another opening. I sighed as I tasted tobacco and the rye-and-coke he had been drinking. His tongue flirted with mine as one of his hands held my chin immobile and the other searched my back. He was looking for a way to get me out of my clothes.

"Umph," I told him. He chivalrously withdrew his tongue. "You'll never find it, man. You can put on some music and I'll do a striptease for you." I slid away from him, reaching around myself to find the zipper that could free my nipples to drink in the fresh air and the gaze of a suitor.

"Slut," he grinned, rolling the word around on his tongue. He fiddled with the dial on the radio until he found a station that played rock classics. "Meanwhile," he promised, "I'll just do this." And before I could guess his next move, one of his hands had deftly pulled up the hem of my skirt and unhooked my garters while he lifted me with the other hand. He found the elastic of my panties and pulled them down, exposing my damp and startled cunt. I hadn't expected him to be so eager.

The nasal voice of a teen idol of yesteryear filled the car with the drama of frustrated love as Barry tickled my clit for an instant, then plunged two fingers as deeply into me as they would go. "Oh!" I gasped, feeling like a teenage girl who is finally experiencing It, the long-awaited rite of passage. His fingers felt large and male inside me, intrusive but friendly. In the dim light from the moon and stars, Barry's grin looked toothy and feral.

"Spread," he ordered, and I spread my legs apart, leaning back on the seat. His fingers wiggled obscenely inside me, checking out every fold and crevice they could find. My clit was in full salute. "You like that, don't you, bad girl?" he prompted.

This was not what I expected. I was about to come, partly from sheer surprise. "Oh, Barry," I gasped, realizing that resistance was probably futile, even if I could summon up the will for it.

He fucked me to a driving beat, stroking my pussy and my mind at once, making me realize that yes, this was what I really wanted. Part of me rejoiced that he was not in salon mode, not schmoozing a customer nor patronizing a lady-friend. Strangely enough, my very wet pussy recognized something man-to-man in his very direct style. I moaned.

"You can come, Lee," he urged. His use of my name made me feel even more exposed, if that was possible. "I want you to. Come hard, make noise. You can hold on to me if you need to."

Like I was going over the rapids, my cunt spasmed over and over. I clutched his shoulder as I held his fingers inside me and wailed along with the radio. Barry chuckled, and this set off another wave of explosions inside me. For a moment of suspended time, I felt as if I could never stop coming. The winding down had a seductive charm of its own, like a buildup in reverse.

Barry's fingers lingered inside me as if they had found a new home, a place where they would never again be strangers. With the pleasurable shiver of a girl watching a monster looming over her on the big screen of the drive-in, I realized the truth of that word, *never*. In a small queer community, carnal knowledge lasts a lifetime. What lust has brought together, let no gossiping mouth sunder.

"Pussy. Cunt. Snatch. Honeypot," mused Barry, trying out the words. "Fascinating, honey. I could get hooked on it. It gets hungry, doesn't it?"

I laughed in answer. "Yeah, it does," he asserted fondly. "I wanted to get you off first, hard, so we could take our time. Not too much, though. You wanna play with my lollipop?"

I could hardly refuse at that point without being too rude, even for a totally out dyke. And I still felt like a dyke, I realized. This whole scene felt too confusing to analyze.

His cock—or *meat*, as I thought all the queens liked to call it—seemed to be an average length, but thicker than most, though I wasn't sure my memories of other specimens were reliable. I was afraid to take it in my mouth without a covering, not because the texture or the expected taste might put me off, but because I was terrified of the kind of operatic death that in the 1950s was only associated with car crashes.

With a kind of elegant reluctance, Barry showed me a small packet which had apparently materialized out of thin air, opened it with his teeth, and smoothed latex over his hardness. *It's for me*, I thought, like a girl who finally gets the phone call she has waited for all weekend.

I stroked it, trying to imitate his boldness and confidence. "Aww," he grunted. "Girlfriend, I want to put it in you. Let's go in the back."

My vague memories of scrambling over the front seat of a family sedan didn't seem to apply to the current setting. I opened the front door on my side, stepped onto welcoming prairie sod, opened the back door, and slid in to find Barry there before me. In a flurry of moving arms and legs, our clothes came off and landed on the floor and the front seat.

In silvery moonlight, I finally saw the alien hairy chest of my friend Barry, who was really a guy from head to foot. He stared with honest amusement at my small, firm breasts with their hard red nipples. He couldn't resist holding them, bouncing them gently, tickling and then rolling my nipples between his fingers and then his teeth. My reactions seemed to amuse him as much as the feel of my flesh. "You wanta ride my stallion, baby?" he suggested.

"Sure," I consented, wondering whether "safe" and "sane" ever really applied to this activity, even in its most traditional forms.

Barry lay on the seat, gazing up at me like Romeo watching

Juliet on her balcony. I spread my obliging pussy lips apart, and settled carefully down on his love-engine. Even though I had just come, his solid warmth inside me was so electrifying that I felt as if my skin must have a neon glow. I moved slowly at first, then eased into a trot and then a gallop, matching his groans with my own. When he came, I squeezed him as hard as I could. Before long, I was doing that uncontrollably as I erupted like a volcano.

He held me against his chest as our breathing returned to normal. "Uh, Barry," I asked, wanting to know how the mood of the evening would translate into a new relationship—or not. "Are we still queer? Like, gay and lesbian?"

His guffaws bounced me so hard that I sat up to look at him. "The word is *bi,* baby." He sang, "Bi-bi, baby, bi-bi." I was afraid of that conclusion.

Barry raised his head to study me. "Well, if we're going to have a conversation about it, do you mind if I have another smoke?"

I sighed. "I don't like it, but I don't want to say no. You're killing yourself, I hope you know, but if you crave it, go ahead." He kissed me with a flourish before reaching into the front seat for his cigarettes.

With all the windows rolled down, the Oldsmobile felt like a very open space or a nondiscriminating orifice. Like the pussy of a slut. I wondered if I would feel so overwhelmed by shame at some future moment that I would swear aloud in the privacy of my apartment.

The healthy smell of green things, the smell of a prairie sum- mer, was all around us like a blessing. "Lee," he began. I could see that Barry was in an intellectual space I could recognize. "You don't want to get married and have babies, do you?"

I shuddered. At least this question was easy. "Hell no."

"Then do you think we've both turned straight? Us? And now we'll be turned off by all the luscious booty at the club because we're not queer anymore?"

In spite of myself, I remembered Gail in bed, as distinct from Gail in other places. Some of the memories had not lost their charm. "It doesn't seem likely," I said hopefully.

"There you go, dear," he said quaintly, a prairie farm boy who had come to the city to discover a life of sin. He held me comfortably, letting me visualize him with the next twink in his life—dancing, flirting, even fucking vulgarly in the men's john. Was I jealous? Not a bit. As the old saying goes, enough is as good as a feast. I knew I could be satisfied as long as I had mine.

"You still wanta go for brunch?" I asked coyly.

"Only if I can go with you," he answered.

KIDNAPPED

Debra Hyde

The moment should've passed routinely enough: Lydia, standing by the driver's side door, fumbling around in her purse, struggling to jam her wallet back inside while searching out her cars keys. She paused and leaned against the car, pinning the purse between it and her. She ran her hand through her hair in exasperation. "Fucking pain in the ass car keys," Lydia fumed as she fumbled.

Yes, at most it should've been a crude, clumsy moment. At most, it should've looked like a harried woman with mussed-up hair at her inept worst.

Lydia, certainly, wasn't thinking of anything besides her truant car keys. She paused and looked up, toward the doors of the ATM kiosk. Had she left them in there? On the counter, maybe, when she had endorsed her check and stuffed it in a bank envelope?

"Christ, don't tell me," she muttered to herself. She reached for her wallet, resigned to returning to the kiosk for a look-see.

The look-see became a no-show. Suddenly, the sounds of running feet, the rustle of clothing, and a threatening "Get her!" rushed her. And surrounded her and grabbed her and held her. Several arms and hands pinned her between bodies, big bodies. Someone forced a hood over her head. Then the voice again. "Quick! Get to the van before anyone sees us."

Instinctively, Lydia began to scream. A strong hand clamped over her mouth. It jammed against her nose. Smarting pain brought tears to her eyes. Lydia blinked them back as the voice connected to the hand hissed, "Quiet, bitch, or we'll hurt you."

"Yeah," came another voice. "We *like* hurting." Then it cackled maniacally.

The two men hustled her along. Pinned by their grip and robbed of sight, Lydia, stumbling, followed their rough lead. Panicked, she tried to scream again, but the sounds of her cries rang mostly in her head. They didn't make it past the hood and the hand that held her face captive. "No noise, bitch!" the hissing voice commanded. He gripped her arm but before she could even think to struggle, he seized her by the breast and squeezed it. Hard. This time, she cried out in pain.

"Like my friend said, we like to hurt." The hand of the hissing voice twisted her tit to prove its point. "Behave!" Which sounded like a final warning to Lydia. Made meek, she collapsed in the men's arms and whimpered in puffy, panicked little breaths.

The men hauled Lydia along, half dragging, half carrying her. The man behind her smelled familiar—Right Guard, she realized, as the image of a high school beau flashed through her mind, an old boyfriend who had used the same deodorant.

Is this my life flashing before my eyes, she wondered?

Other odd realizations hit her as she was being dragged: a shoe threatening to slip from her foot, her thigh-high stocking beginning to droop. She clenched her toes to keep the shoe on her foot; she couldn't rescue the stocking.

Rescue. Who would rescue her?

No one apparently. Over the scurrying hustle of her abductors, Lydia heard a van's metal doors creak open. Her captors lifted her off the ground and practically tossed her into the vehicle. A mattress met her body as she fell to the floor. She heard the doors slam shut and the men settle in around her as the van lurched into gear. The sounds of metal objects shifting and the odors of old oil, chemicals, and solvents told her she was in the back of a work vehicle. Perhaps a plumber's or a painter's van?

But before she could move and react, the men were upon her again, grabbing her wrists and ankles. Lydia fought, squirmed, struggled.

"Who are you?" she blurted through the hood. Her voice echoed inside it, amplified by it.

"Do you hear that?" the cackler asked. "Who are you?" he mimicked sarcastically. Lydia imagined a sneer on his face.

"Well one thing's for sure," hissing voice said. "She doesn't think she's David Balfour casting off on the Covenant, circa seventeen-fifty-one."

David Balfour. Covenant. 1751.

Her code words! Those were her code words!

Instantly, Lydia relinquished her fear. This wasn't an abduction, but a mock kidnapping and she was its latest "victim." As the van rumbled over the parking lot's speed bumps and bounced her about, she giggled. So this was what it felt like to be kidnapped!

It felt like two men holding her down, tying her hands together, then her ankles. Simple, classic bondage, just like in old black-and-white photos from long ago. Lydia stretched, languorously, catlike, on the mattress. She arched her back, put her best breast forward, hoping to tease her captors. *Maybe,* she thought, *I can get them to come around to my way of seeing things.* Being a do-me kind of woman had its advantages.

"What's in her dossier?"

It was the hissing voice; the one that had provided the code words, only now it was flat and authoritative, smacking of leadership. *Circa 1751. Dossier.* Lydia realized that the voice was intelligent, the brains of the operation. This was the voice whose favor she needed to curry. She worked her way toward him and found the man's legs at mattress's edge. She rubbed her head against them, ever catlike. *Notice me,* she wished. *Don't resist.*

A voice she hadn't heard before spoke. "Here. Take a look. I'm too busy driving." Another man, she figured.

The hissing man—Brains—pushed Lydia back onto the mattress. "Stay put," he commanded her, not giving an inch in acknowledgment. Papers rustled.

"Let's see what we have here," he said. More paper rustling. "Willful, stubborn brat. Always weaseling into your good graces."

"Yeah and weaseling all over your legs too," Cackle interjected.

"We'll break her of that. What else? Let's see. Limits, limits...where's her limits?"

Limits? The word caught Lydia's attention. Her boyfriend had filled out the form one night while she lay prone in his bed, tied down and blindfolded. She remembered what he had said when he reached the limits section of the form. "Limits. Hmm. Let's see. Shit play. Fucking. Unprotected oral. Safe shots okay. Gee, that all?"

"All" wasn't much. Lydia shuddered then at the lack of limits and she shuddered now. The playing field, her boyfriend had decided, was wide open. Which served her right, he'd claimed, since she'd badgered him for weeks to sign her up as a victim.

He hadn't wanted to, but, as he'd complained, "Sometimes the only way to get a brat off your back is to give in."

Now, Cackle spoke, from alongside her. "Gee, except for the no-fucking limit, she sounds like a regular party girl. Guess that means I can do this."

Lydia felt Cackle's hands at her blouse. "No!" she shouted as he forcefully tore it open. "No? Did you say no?" he taunted as he slipped a hand into her bra and cupped her tit. He petted her clumsily, grabbing and squeezing her breast like some crass frat boy hell-bent on a drunken fuck. Her nipple went hard at his touch.

"Nice, very nice," he cooed in breathy lust.

The sound of his voice sent a shiver up Lydia's spine. And it sounded familiar. Where had she heard that before?

"Too bad we can't fuck her," Cackle complained. "But I can do this, right?"

Lydia felt Cackle's crotch press into her face. Denim, she smelled denim and, through it, the faint whiff of sweaty balls. Cackle's raging hard-on pressed against her lips, shielded only by the armor of his pant's zipper and her hood. Lydia felt besieged, powerless to push this man off her face. And then he started humping her face. He slid back and forth over her face as his hips gyrated. Cackle's breathing grew ragged, as if her face was the means for a hasty jacking off.

"Safe shots," he muttered. "Yeah, that's good. I wanna shoot all over this bitch's tits."

Humiliation rushed through Lydia, paralyzing her. Cackle was a creep, a real pervert in her book, the kind of guy she'd cross the street to avoid. The kind of guy, if he approached her at Hellfire or Paddles, she'd scoff at and say, "Not in a million years, not even if you were the last man on earth." She bet he even had thin, greasy hair, yellowed leering teeth, and weasel slits for eyes.

But here he was, humping her face. Cackle grabbed her by

the back of the head and pressed her forward into his crotch, making Lydia puff for every breath. *Horrid, he's horrid,* she thought. She thanked her lucky stars for the miracle of thick denim and Lycra hoods.

A hand slipped into her bra, cupping her breast. Not Cackle's—he was too busy face-fucking her. Brains? It had to be Brains's hand. The hand weighed her breast with a bounce, as if it was some grocery store grapefruit. It even squeezed the fruit for ripeness.

"Jeez, I don't know what you're getting so worked up about," Brains sneered to his humping friend as he removed his hand. "She's just your basic B-cup. Nothing to write home about."

Lydia sat there, taking it, shocked. She liked her breasts. Sure, they weren't centerfold breasts, but then a centerfold's breasts weren't either. The crotch pulled away.

"Yeah, well, they'll do in a pinch."

Cackle slipped his hands into each bra cup, found Lydia's nipples, and squeezed unforgivingly. Lydia screamed and thrashed about, trying to escape his cruelties. Cackle laughed and let go. He'd proved his point.

For a time, they rode in silence. The van's every little movement made it feel like a ship swaying on the high seas. So far, her captors hadn't really stressed her badly. Mostly, they'd grossed her out. Especially Cackle. *Creep,* she thought.

A hand placed itself on her knee. The hand was big, encompassing, and warm. She hoped it was Brains's. She readily preferred him to Cackle and she imagined him as a Harrison Ford type. *How bad could that be?* she asked herself.

"We're almost there," Brains told her. (Yes, Brains!) "You know you haven't placed many limits in our way, don't you?"

"My boyfriend did that," Lydia responded.

"So what. You signed the paper. You consented." Brains

went silent for a moment, then added, "I'll give your boyfriend credit. He's plenty generous."

The hand traveled up Lydia's skirt, found the cleft between her legs and crept under her panties.

"Real generous." The tenor of Brains's voice softened but it did not grow any more gentle. Lydia knew the sound of that voice; it was the sound of a man pondering all the erotic possibilities that stood before him. It was the sound of a man getting a hard-on.

"Just because my boyfriend's generous doesn't mean I'm gonna be," she declared. "I'm not that easy."

"Bullshit!" Brains shot back, grabbing whatever portion of cunt he could and pinching it. "You'll do whatever we want you to do! Understand?"

He had her by the labia, just as hard as Cackle had had her nipples. Lydia bellowed through the pain, wanting it to stop.

"Understand?" Brains demanded an answer.

"Yes! Yes, I do! Just let go, damn it!"

A slap shot across her hooded face. "Don't swear at us, you bitch! And don't tell us what to do either." Cackle again. His slap was more humiliating than painful and Lydia went silent, the blush of embarrassment hot on her face. She hated Cackle, she decided right there and then, but she obeyed because she wanted the pinching to stop.

Sure enough, Brains let go and Lydia cried out as her cunt lips throbbed in pained relief. He instructed Cackle to spread her thighs.

The bondage prevented much of a spread but it allowed enough. Brains pulled his hands from beneath her panties and started patting her pussy in sure little slaps, slaps meant to arouse. Cackle's hands—with their long, skinny fingers—held her thighs, occasionally squeezing them. Being held there by two men, one holding her down while the other slapped her pussy, was more than Lydia could fight. Especially since it felt so good. She moaned. She fell into the mounting swell of arousal, of orgasm nearing, that feeling of all sensations swirling and coalescing and tightening and exploding and pulsing. Coming, she was coming. Her moan had transformed itself into the cries of ecstasy as Brains slowed his slapping to a light caress.

"Do it again," Cackle instigated. "Come on. Do it again."

"Yeah," the driver shot back from the front seat, "she came in two minutes flat. If I know anything about sluts, she's good for another one."

Brains laughed and started again, this time, rubbing her clit. "No, please no," Lydia whined. "It's so sensitive." She hated how vulnerable her clit was after orgasm, how easy a target for torture it became. "No?" Brains teased. "Did you hear that? She said no. Like she has a choice."

A slap on the thigh and a "Bitch!" came from Cackle. Then again. And again, over and over. Each slap burned into Lydia's thighs, reminding her of her boyfriend's choice hairbrush, reminding her how he'd use it when he could no longer take her brattiness. Now this creep was slapping her, belittling her with verbal slights as he went. "Bitch! Cunt! Slut!" He used all the words that her boyfriend didn't have the balls to call her, even when she deserved it. But this creep, he could say it. She resented him even as he humiliated her. *I'll get you,* she silently swore. *Somehow, I'll get back at you.*

But Brains's touch was another thing—trying and difficult, but ultimately not a thing to rebel against. Yes, her clit felt raw. Yes, it screamed *Don't touch me!* But it also complied with Brains's actions. It responded to him, working its way to another peak despite the discomfort. That was, after all, its function.

And it overwhelmed Lydia. Everything overwhelmed her.

Brains masturbating her, Cackle humiliating her with every slap, the burn of those slaps, the raw edge of her clit, her conflict about her captors, her clit speaking its own mind. Which finally shouted and Lydia followed in tandem, crying out as she came.

When all was said and done, when hands left her and Lydia recovered, she was aware of two things: the driver's voice claiming "She had to work at that one," and the fact that the van had stopped.

"Come on, let's string her up." Driver's voice, deep and resonant.

They dragged her across a hardwood floor, if the sound of their steps was any clue, then plopped her down. Her wrists and ankles were seized and relieved of their rope. But leather cuffs went into place and something else, between her ankles. A spreader bar. The sound of chains went with them. She rested in her captors' arms as a metallic sound commenced. It was the crank of a hoist.

Lydia felt her ankles rise. She was being raised up, into suspension. Her legs rose into air, then her torso, then all of her. Lydia had no real idea how high up she was, only that her hair and arms dangled downward. She felt a slight sway to the suspension, a gentle sensation and not what she expected of such a dramatic position.

Something cold slipped under the waistband of her skirt.

"We gotta strip her down. Too many clothes," Brains said.

"Just remember what Medusa wants," Cackle reminded. "We don't want cross her."

Medusa? Who was that?

Brains grunted an acknowledgment, then pressed the cold object into Lydia's skirt. Which began to rip. A knife! She tried to imagine what it looked like as it pulled along her skirt and tore it away. It took only seconds for Brains to cut her skirt in half and remove it. He slapped her pantied ass with the flat of the knife.

"That's going to be nice to play with," he commented off-handedly.

Cackle wasn't so coy. "I'd like to shove my dick up it and fuck it."

"You wanna fuck everything," Brains shot back as he placed the knife under Lydia's blouse, ripped it up the back and then down each arm. Lydia tensed as it traveled across her body. She expected he'd continue until she was fully exposed.

But he didn't. He stopped when the blouse fell from her and, instead, pulled her panties down—well, up—to her thighs, exposing her round rump.

Brains patted it soundly. "Nice ass. Grade-A."

"Choice cut for a spanker like you," Driver joked.

"Takes one to know one," Brains shot back. *Sheesh*, Lydia thought, *they sound like grade school kids on the playground.*

"Hey, let's take turns with her," Driver said.

Take turns with her. The words made Lydia seize up with fear. Take turns with her. How far would that go?

"First dibs!" Cackle declared. To Lydia's absolute fright and disgust, she heard his zipper in motion. The sound of condom dispensing followed. *Oh god, no*, she thought. Then she uttered the words as she felt Cackle's creepy hands at her cheeks, rolling the hood down over the bridge of her nose.

"Better let me hold that in place," Brain said. Lydia felt his touch at the back of her head, gathering the hood's drawstrings tight.

"You just wanna watch," Cackle bantered.

"Hey, front row seats." Brain's voice was ear level; Lydia realized he was kneeling next to her. "And you better give me a good show," he told Lydia. That breathy, hard-up voice of his was back.

"Yeah, baby, you better give good head," Cackle said as he pressed the tip of his cock to her lips. "Open up, cunt."

"No," Lydia said, tight-lipped like a ventriloquist. "No."

Brains tugged on the drawstrings. "You better take that cock if you know what's good for you."

"Nnnn-Nnnn."

"You bitch!" Cackle shouted. "You're gonna open up!" To prove it, he grabbed her clit and pinched it. Shocked by sudden, searing pain, Lydia screamed. And found Cackle's cock stuffing itself into her mouth. *I'll bite you, you bastard,* her thoughts flared, but Cackle stopped pinching and started face-fucking her, his arms clenching her around the waist as she dangled. Lydia felt his meat slide back and forth, short and stocky and, to her relief, not at all an effort to accommodate. As she felt the pain in her clit fade to a dull throb, she heard Brains reward her with a "That's a good girl."

"Too bad she fought me," Cackle commented. "With her pussy practically in my face, I was gonna eat cunt while I fucked. But no more Mr. Nice Guy for her."

But he did explore her pussy with his hand while he face-fucked her. His fingers parted her lips; she felt them at her crevice, brushing over her clit, making her shudder. He dipped into her depths and Lydia could hear her lips smack in wetness. The sound made all thoughts of biting his cock vanish.

"Yeah, too bad. She smells *real* good."

Returning his hand to her waist, Cackle stepped up his face-fucking with a "Nice throat," comment. Lydia, dangling, felt the air begin to rush in her ears, the drool pooling, then spilling from her mouth. The face-fucking took on a noisy slurping, the sounds of a heavy blowjob. And Cackle was getting off on it. "Yeah, cunt, that's the way. Nice and wet."

He began to pummel her faster, accenting every stab with a

staccato grunt. Then, he wrenched himself free of her mouth. She heard him peel the condom off; she heard his hand sliding back and forth over his cock. Cackle grabbed her pussy again, this time clutching it with one hand while his grunts became wheezy and weak.

Then, he was there. He cried out once as he peaked, then muttered a sick, perverted "Oh yeah," for each of the four shots of come that hit Lydia, right between her breasts. It was runny stuff and, as she felt Brain loosen his hold on the drawstrings, Cackle's spunk dripped onto the shelf of her chin. There, it stayed. No one made an effort to wipe her clean. Brains simply rolled her panties back into place, the hood, too, letting the spunk seep into the Lycra fabric.

"Feel better now?" he asked Cackle.

Lydia gasped. Cackle's hands were back inside her bra, feeling her up. "Oh yeah, I feel better," he answered; then, directing his comments to her tits, he mumbled "Nice, very nice." That perverted lust was back in his voice, sending chills along Lydia's spine. She knew she'd heard that very line somewhere before but where? She wanted to wrack her brains and find out, but Driver spoke up instead.

"We better get cracking. Five minutes until Medusa."

The sound of the hoist resumed and, as the rope went slack, Brains and Driver took Lydia in their arms and returned her to standing. Lydia felt instantly unsteady.

"You're okay," Brains said. "We'll hold on to you. Lean on me."

Lydia did, thankfully. She was right about feeling safe with Brains: he had a heart. The pleasant scent of his deodorant lulled her. Yeah, Brains was okay. The fact that he hadn't jerked off on her meant a lot too.

Her reprieve, though, was temporary. Once Lydia had regained her land legs, the men set to work about her. Cackle dragged a chair over, its legs complaining against the wood floor, and set it near her. Brains guided her to the chair and issued a curt "Sit." A length of rope settled around her neck. Sensing danger, Lydia hollered an instinctive "No!" and tried to bolt from the chair, but Brains pushed her back into place. "Don't worry," he explained calmly. "It's not a hangman's noose. We just want you in a certain position. It's safe; you'll see."

Driver began to direct Lydia. "Raise your legs up. Yeah, that's it. Now slip your arm under your legs to keep them up."

As Lydia complied, she felt a pair of handcuffs catch and capture her wrists. Cold, metal handcuffs. She winced as they touched her skin. *They'll warm up,* she told herself. *They always do.*

"Don't panic, we're just attaching the rope to the cuffs," Brains added as Driver tied her down. While he worked the rope onto the cuffs, Lydia felt lengths of rope encircle her ankles, tying her to the legs of the chair. Secured, she assessed the position she found herself in. The rope around her neck drew her head downward, placing stress at the back of her neck, but, at the same time, it eased the stress of keeping her hands in place. It was an odd and uncomfortable position, not truly painful but certainly inflexible. *What can they do to me while I'm like this,* she wondered? *It's not like my ass is sticking out.* The thought brought images of spankings, floggings, and fucking to mind—the kind of gangbang every pervy girl dreamed of, yet feared.

"Let's have a look," Driver said. Lydia instantly figured she was about to find out what they could do to her, but a crinkle of paper and the men agreeing "She's posed as outlined," told her all she was going to know for the moment. They didn't touch her; they didn't taunt her. In fact, she got the distinct impression from their idleness that their time with her might very well be up.

"What are you going to do with me now?" she blurted.

Cackle was the first to laugh and say, "Nothing!" Brains added, "Consider yourself on display." Then, they retreated, leaving her there, alone.

Alone, for the first time in this entire drama. Alone, with no clue to decipher and determine what might come next, with no contact from her captors, with no rapport to sustain. Rapport. Lydia startled at that realization. She had established a rapport with her captors, just like a real kidnap victim. She had stopped bratting around and had submitted to their demands on cue. In her solitude, she missed them, even the creepy Cackle, and she realized that being alone with no clue about what would happen next or when was more than she wanted to bear.

Her solitude ended when the sound of footsteps neared—a woman's well-heeled footsteps. The strong scent of perfume approached as well and settled around Lydia. Other faint footsteps followed, further behind. They sounded soft, as if slippered, and Lydia couldn't tell how many people formed the pitter-patter of those little feet.

"Well, let's see how well my boys did," the woman said. Her voice was sharp, dripping with contempt, and smacked of finishing school culture. Lydia imagined Audrey Hepburn's grace in Cruella De Vil's body. *Medusa,* she surmised.

Again, a paper rattled. Again, the woman spoke. "Hood, handcuffs, rope, position."

"Check." A man's voice, soft, almost effeminate.

"Heels, stockings, panties, bra," Medusa continued.

"Check," the man indicated.

"As instructed, ma'am," a third voice—another woman—confirmed.

"Nice, very nice," Medusa sneered.

Medusa used Cackle's trademark words but emphatically

and without any hint of sliminess. Lydia imagined a wicked, sly grin on the woman's face, then realized that, just like Cackle, the woman wanted to get off. Suddenly, she remembered the reference: a Hitchcock movie, one of his last, where a sadistic murderer pawed his female victims' breasts and drooled the words over them. *Right before he killed them.* Lydia shivered, thankful she hadn't recognized the reference in Cackle's presence.

Medusa interrupted her realization. "Let's toy with our little captive, what do you say?" Soft, cruel laughter came from her attendants.

Another chair was dragged into place, not far from Lydia. Medusa sat down. At least that's what the swish of fabric told Lydia.

"Jake, come crawl over here and find your way up my skirts. I want your tongue to amuse me while Rebecca goes after our little prisoner here."

A breathy, enthusiastic "Yes, ma'am," accompanied the sounds of the man falling to his knees and maneuvering under what sounded like layers of petticoats. The crinkling of stiff fabric punctuated his every move up her legs. She knew he had hit the right spot when Medusa let escape a lusty moan of "Oh yeah."

"Go to it, girl," Medusa commanded. "Let's see you eat muff for lunch today."

Lydia froze, seized by the fact that a woman was going to go down on her. A woman. A woman had never touched her. Something cool slid between her panties and pussy. A dental dam?

Then Rebecca's touch, her mouth. Lydia would know her only by her mouth. It latched itself to Lydia's crotch, chewing on her panties until they were soaked with saliva. It tugged them aside and made way for its tongue, which explored Lydia's folds, her creases, and the rocky hardness of her clit as best it could through the dam. The tongue circled and pressed; it darted in, finding depth. The plastic dam had some give to it and traveled up Lydia's cunt. The woman assaulted every avenue she could find, lapping her length from front to back, even attempting to reach for Lydia's puckered anus. Lydia felt her nipples go hard, aching in arousal. She felt her clit beg for more tongue, her lips swell at the touch of Rebecca's lips, her cunt grow tight and demanding. She was so close.

"Make her come," Medusa commanded, her ever-strong voice still stern but hinting at her own nearing climax. "I want to see her come."

Lydia felt two fingers slip into her and coax her. Rebecca's tongue plowed up her slit to her ready clit, and when tongue reached clit, when it applied a forceful strumming, Lydia could stand no more. She came, bucking in her bondage, as a long cry of ecstasy erupted from her.

And, as her own voice faded, she heard Medusa grunting and grinding in a quieter version of the same delight. Lydia felt fingers leave her slit and peel away the plastic dam. Her hood rolled upward, exposing her mouth and nose. Suddenly, the dam was plastered there, blocking her breathing. She gasped in desperate fear as Rebecca coerced, "You want to breathe? Lick this clean, slut."

Lydia applied a dutiful tongue to the task. Her juices had smeared the dam, juices she now lapped up as the overwhelming scent of sex sent her spinning in objectification. Rebecca pulled the dam away abruptly, leaving Lydia panting and relieved. "Not bad for a cunt," Rebecca observed as she fussed the hood back into place. Lydia flushed with a strange combination of humiliation and quiet pride.

Medusa stood, straightened her clothing, and ordered her people to "dispense with this one." Her attendants removed the ropes and helped Lydia stand. They let her stretch, then led her to another room, this one carpeted and warmer. But they didn't remove the handcuffs, laughing when she asked. Instead, they placed her on a mattress and tied her cuffs to another length of rope. One of them checked her hood, saying, "She can't get at it." Rebecca, it was Rebecca speaking. "You'll be claimed soon. Just lie down and rest."

Lydia heard them move away, presumably for the door, but, just before they left, Rebecca added, "Oh, by the way, you're a tasty cunt. For a straight girl." Lydia blushed fiercely at the dyke's parting shot.

Time passed. How much, Lydia wasn't certain but it was enough to nap by. She woke now and then, vaguely becoming aware before drifting back to sleep.

But she startled awake when a body pressed against her and pushed her flat onto her belly. An arm across her upper back forced her down, the other went between her legs and pried them apart. And, like Rebecca's mouth, it wrested her panties aside. She felt a cock there, at her cleft, ready to take her.

"No! No penetration! Stop!"

"Shut up. It's just me."

It was her boyfriend, and he had his own ideas about what "release the prisoner" meant. He pushed his hard, eager meat up into Lydia. At first she was dry, but she slicked up perfectly. "You feel good," he told her. "The way you do when I make you come a lot before I fuck you." Lydia swooned, too timid to tell him just how right he had it. He was more focused on his cock anyway, noticing her cunt only for what it did for him.

Lydia didn't complain. For all her brattiness, she liked being used and it didn't get much better than being forced awake by the feeling of her man's dick pumping her for all it was worth.

Her boyfriend began grunting with every stroke and he reached under her, searching out her breasts to clutch. He found her bra, squeezed its contents, and held on as his movements grew faster and more frenzied. His breath was against her ear, loud and animalistic. Orgasm was imminent, and abruptly he slammed deep and held himself there. Lydia could feel his cock pulsing, spurting, filling her with the fruits of its labor. Finally, he collapsed on top of her.

Minutes later, he pulled his withering prick from her and hauled himself up off of Lydia. He helped Lydia sit up, then freed her from the bondage—the cuffs, the hood. Her sight was blinded by the return of light but even through the blur, she could see his limp cock in her face. "Lick it clean," he ordered her.

Lydia did, tasting the mélange of his come and her juices, licking its length, top and bottom, taking the time to slather his pubic hair and balls for good measure.

"You look good," her boyfriend commented as he watched her clean. "We're going to have to do this again sometime."

As he spoke, Lydia remembered the feel of Brains, his grip, his cupping her "B-cup" breasts, his torturing touch as he stroked her into coming. She remembered creepy Cackle with his pinching and his humping and his coming all over her. A familiar heat ignited between her legs and she knew her boyfriend was right. She envisioned whips and paddles, cocks and circle jerks. She envisioned Rebecca, this time bringing friends and passing her around among them.

The answer was simple and, smiling, Lydia agreed. *Yes, we'll have to do this again. Soon. Real soon.*

SATISFACTION GUARANTEED

Kristina Wright

The store was called Heart's Desire and I had never been inside, even though I passed it every day on my walk to work. Monday through Friday, I studied the store window from under lowered lashes. I always hurried past, as if something—perhaps that large double-headed dildo in the window—would reach out and grab me.

I don't know what made me slow down one Friday afternoon after work. I don't know why I took a deep breath and stopped. Maybe I was ready to find out what I'd been missing. Maybe I was just psychotically hormonal. Whatever the reason, I finally opened the door and went inside.

I expected porno soundtrack music and shag carpet. Instead, there was a soft classical piece playing and hardwood floors. The displays in the store were as garish as the window displays, but somehow they didn't seem nearly so salacious now that I had ventured inside.

The store appeared to be empty, but there was a doorway

behind the counter and I assumed someone was back there, sticker-pricing dildos. I giggled.

"If you're this happy already, you may be in the wrong place," a masculine voice said from behind me.

I jumped, nearly taking out a display of furry handcuffs and restraints. "I'm sorry," I mumbled.

I glanced at this weirdo who would work in a sex shop. Surprisingly, he didn't look so weird. Six two, at least, with brown hair that was long enough to brush his shoulders and a nose that looked as if it had been broken. I resisted the urge to run my finger over the bump.

"I was wondering when you would get up the nerve to actually come in."

"You were watching me?"

He nodded. "Every day for the past couple of months. You always look over here as if you're going to cross yourself and say a Hail Mary for whatever dirty thoughts you're thinking."

It wasn't far from the truth, but it still annoyed me. "Maybe this was a mistake."

He grinned. "Easy, sweetheart. I'm just teasing. Have a look around."

He disappeared through the door behind the counter and I was blissfully alone, surrounded by sex toys of every size, shape and color. I wandered the aisles, my hands tucked in my jean pockets, not having the nerve to touch anything.

Some of it was lurid. Some of it was a little scary. But some of it, I hated to admit, was arousing. Edible creams, nipple clamps, butt plugs, vibrators for every occasion—I'd been missing a lot. The closest I'd ever gotten to a sex toy was a brief experiment with a rather well-endowed cucumber while I was drunk on cheap wine.

"See anything you like?" It was him again, sneaking up behind me.

I wanted to be mad, but I almost laughed. "Do you try to intimidate all your customers?"

"Am I intimidating you?"

He looked so boyish and innocent I did laugh this time. "Nope, not at all." As if to prove my point, I picked up a massive purple dildo and hefted it in my hand. "Does this come in a larger size?"

"How big do you want it?"

My grin wavered. I wasn't sure if we were still teasing or if he was making a pass. While I wanted to be indignant about him making suggestive comments, I couldn't work up the necessary anger. I was in a sex shop and he was cute; it seemed reasonable to flirt a little.

I could feel myself blushing. "I was just kidding. Which one is most popular?"

He tucked a feather duster in the back pocket of his jeans and scanned the row of dildos. "Try this one," he said, taking a pearly pink dildo from the bottom shelf. "It's our best seller, even if it's not the most impressive."

I studied the modest dildo dubiously. "It's not very big."

He laughed. "Bigger isn't necessarily better."

"I'll take your word for it." I followed him to the register and he rang me up.

"Pretty name, Kylie McCullough," he said.

"Thanks." I wondered if anyone would be able to guess what was in the plain white bag.

"I'm Jeff." He leaned across the counter. "In case you need anything else. Anything at all."

His tone was so serious, I did a double take. I'd led a tame life, with just a couple of serious boyfriends and a fair number of orgasms—many of them self-induced. My sex life had been pretty steady since college, but nothing to write home about.

Here was a guy who sold sex toys for a living and knew which dildos would give the best results.

"Do you think you could show me how to use this thing?" Clearly, I was possessed by a sex goddess, but once the words were out, I had no desire to take them back.

His eyes went wide for a fraction of a second. I waited for him to say no. Instead, he nodded. "Sure, sweetheart."

He walked to the door, flipped the OPEN sign to CLOSED and turned the lock. "I'm yours for an hour."

I was practically trembling as he led me to the back room. Shelves lined three walls; a desk was crammed in the corner. The shelves were packed with boxes and opened cartons, sex toys and other assorted sundries spilling out.

Jeff didn't waste any time. He spun me around until my ass was against the desk. His grin was as wicked as my thoughts. "You sure about this?"

I nodded. "Show me."

I shimmied out of my skirt and panties and hopped up on the desk. Truth be told, I wasn't thinking about the dildo, I was thinking about the sizable lump in his pants. But I wasn't that kind of girl. Not yet, anyway.

He nudged my knees open a bit farther with his hip. He held the dildo up for my inspection. "This one has little ridges. They'll rub your clit when it slides in and out of you."

I spread my legs a bit wider without him telling me to. He produced a bottle of lubricant and squirted a dollop on the toy's tip. The first contact of the jellied rubber dildo and chilled lube against my warm cunt made me jump. "It's cold!"

"Relax. It'll warm up."

Slowly, carefully, he slid the head of the dildo inside me. I could see the rest of it quivering in his hand as I wiggled.

"How does that feel?"

"Not deep enough," I mumbled, sliding my ass forward on the desk. "I need more."

He laughed. "The lady wants to get fucked, she'll get fucked."

He braced one hand on my hip and I leaned back on my hands and closed my eyes as he started to fuck me with my new pink toy. I could feel his fingers bump against my clit on every downstroke and the combination of cool dildo and warm skin made me whimper.

"The great thing about these rubber dildos," he said, "is how flexible they are. They can really rub your G-spot if you angle them correctly." He demonstrated and I moaned.

"Like I said, the bumps are great for clitoral stimulation." He angled the dildo down into me and I could feel every bump on the way down.

"Shut up and fuck me," I gasped.

He did. Alternating strokes, he drove the dildo into me again and again until I almost forgot it wasn't a real cock. It warmed to my body temperature and seemed to swell inside me, though I knew it was really my cunt becoming engorged as I approached orgasm.

I opened my eyes and the sight of Jeff standing between my spread legs, my juices glistening on his fingers as he fucked me, his cock still hard in his pants, pushed me over the edge. I held on to his wrist with a death grip as I moaned and came, while he kept fucking me hard.

"Enough, enough," I finally whimpered.

My cunt made a wet sucking sound as he pulled the dildo out. "Well?"

"That was..." I paused for a moment to catch my breath. "Amazing. I've never come like that before." I was pretty sure I'd left a puddle on his desk. "Thanks."

"My pleasure. I better go ahead and reopen the store. Take your time."

I waited to get dressed until he left me. I was right: there was a wet spot on the desk. I decided to leave it as an autograph.

I wiped the dildo down with the hem of my shirt and tossed it in the bag. Back out in the store, Jeff was talking to a young woman who couldn't decide whether to look at him or the sex toys he was pointing at.

She spotted me coming out of the back and her eyes went wide.

"Thanks for your assistance," I said.

Jeff smiled. "Enjoy your purchase."

"I will." As I walked past the woman, I stage-whispered, "This store has the best customer service."

TUBING THE BRULE

Reen Guierre

The bus ride to the Brule River was beautiful. It was mid-August, and already an occasional tree had been transformed to red by the cool nights. The last five miles on a washboard dirt road, however, were a drag. Cami had to pee and the guy she had to sit next to smiled beneath his shades every time she looked in his direction. She had never been inner-tubing before, but like all risky outdoor fun, it seemed to come with a degree of sacrifice.

Finally the bus pulled to a stop and Derek (she thought that's what he'd said his name was) got into the aisle and motioned for her to go ahead of him. She slipped past him and pushed ahead, trying to put as many people between them as possible. Once out of the bus, she made a beeline for the restroom, which turned out to be a stone building with an outhouse pit. Well, at least there was toilet paper. *Just don't look down,* she said to herself.

Cami, Thea and Matt had all signed up for this river trip with

the thought of maybe hooking up with guys. They had all gradu-
ated high school together and this was their final fling before
going off to college. As she exited the outhouse she caught sight
of Matt. It appeared he was already engaged in friendly banter
with a tall, deeply tanned, twentysomething. She approached
them and introduced herself to the tall stranger. The guy's name
was Pete and upon hearing him speak she thought, *No question
about it, he's Matt's type.*

Now where was Thea? Cami shaded her eyes with her hand
and began a sweep, seeking out her friend. She spotted her at
three o'clock talking to two guys. Cami waved to catch her
eye, but Thea only waved back. A man's voice coming from
a megaphone said, "We rendezvous two hours from now for
lunch. You won't miss the signs. The river is very calm this time
of year. Choose a buddy and travel in groups of two or more.
Gear up."

He was so close, Cami felt him standing behind her before
he spoke. "I'll be your buddy," he said. She turned around and
it was Derek, with his shades pushed up over his head. His eyes
were really nice. They were soft and smoky. Why hadn't she
given him a chance before? He was actually quite good-looking.
There was something different about him, but hey, she liked
different.

"Okay, cool," she replied.

It was pleasurable to float down the river at a slow pace, checking out nature and stuff. That weightless, floating feeling made
Cami forget everything that had aggravated her earlier. Derek
had his shades back on and a perpetual grin on his mug. He playfully paddled over to bump inner tubes with her every now and
then. "Will you steer me if I close my eyes?" she asked him.

"Sure."

She closed her eyes and became aware that she no longer

heard the voices of anyone else. It was lovely just listening to the birds and moving water. The dappled sun moved over her eyelids, making her see the color red. She floated contentedly with her fingertips draped in the cool, iron-colored water. As if to wake her out of a dream, there was a jolt as they hit ground. She opened her eyes to see Derek getting up out of his tube.

"Wassup?" she asked.

"I have to pee."

"Go in the water. Doesn't everyone do that?"

"I would if I had my trunks, but I'm wearing cutoffs."

"Whatever," she said, and he disappeared into the woods.

She waited a long time, but he didn't come back. He must be taking a crap, she thought. She didn't have a waterproof watch so she wasn't certain, but it must have been fifteen minutes since he left by now.

She called his name. A muffled reply came back. She pulled the tubes fully up onto the shore and set out to find him. She called him and followed his voice to the top of a small cliff. He was lying facedown, sunning himself on a rock with his cutoffs pulled only part way up so almost his whole ass was showing.

"What the fuck? Are you okay?" Cami demanded.

"My jeans are so tight from the water, I can't get them up. I decided to dry off a little bit and try again," Derek said in a small voice.

"You are joking. This is the worst come-on ever!" She reached down and gave his ass a good slap. Instead of jumping to attention, like she thought he would, he lay there motionless and moaned a little. She looked at the handprint that was beginning to form on his right cheek and realized how beautiful his naked butt looked on the rock warmed by the sunlight. It was obvious he wanted more so she slapped his cheeks, first one, then the other, until they were warm. The sharp noise disturbed the natural sound of the river and woods, even though every-thing else felt so right. Her hand was beginning to sting, but his sexy moaning kept her going and with each contact she began to feel that familiar, bright-hot sensation throughout her groin. He seemed invigorated, judging by his breathing. She stopped to survey the damage and his whole ass was bright red. There were dirt and pine needles stuck to him, which must have made her slaps all the more painful. Derek turned over and said, "Let me taste you."

She really didn't need any more coaxing than that. Cami rolled her shorts and panties in one twisted wad down to her ankles and kicked them aside. She sat on the warm rock facing the sun and watched him position himself between her legs. He lay on his stomach again and she could see that his ass was still glowing. He tongued her like he was tasting something delicious and the experience was enhanced by the direct sunlight. There was no comparison between having sex in a well-lit room and being in full sun. She could study every little shine of saliva on his tongue as he dabbed it gently until the movement of her hips told him she wanted it faster.

He pulled back and said, "I don't have a condom, and I'm assuming you don't either."

She actually did, but she wanted him to keep going. "No," she said in a voice a couple of notes higher than her usual. He continued tonguing her with long licks and flat circles. She was glad she was a girl when she came in shudders and released her calls of pleasure into the air.

After a few minutes they decided they must get back with the group. She was trying to untangle her wet underwear and he said, "Skip those," and tossed them into a bush.

She reached for her shorts and he snatched them away, too. "Derek, damn you, I have to wear something!"

He produced a jackknife from his front pocket and proceeded to cut a small hole in the crotch of her shorts. He handed them back to her with that same smile she had seen on the bus. She also noticed that his shorts did, in fact, go up without a problem.

Getting back into the cold water was chilly at first, but after a while they were laughing and playing again in their tubes. When her tube spun backward the current would force cold water into the tiny hole he'd made in her shorts. It was a little shock every time and kept her attention focused there.

No one batted an eyelash when she and Derek arrived late. Apparently, they weren't the only ones who'd stopped along the way. They had a grilled meal of hot dogs and hamburgers, sitting near Thea and one of her beaus. Derek, she learned to her delight, went to a college in southern Minnesota that was only sixty miles from hers in Wisconsin. An hour was doable, for sure.

Eventually, Matt and Pete showed up looking kind of cold from being wet in the cooler afternoon air. They couldn't stop smiling, and Cami wondered what, exactly, they had done together.

The bus arrived to collect them all and take them to Bayfield. She and Derek sat in the same seats, with him on the aisle. He pulled a jacket from a backpack he'd left on the bus and tossed it over their laps. Before long his hand was under the jacket searching for the hole he'd made in her shorts. His index finger pushed through and found her clit. He touched it ever so lightly and then urged her to scoot forward so he could finger-fuck her. It was all she could do to stay quiet as the urgency screamed in her head. He pulled his finger out and brought it back to her clit, which he then rubbed with her own juices. She came quietly, only tensing up, so no one could tell what was happening. She opened her eyes to see him wearing a very satisfied grin. He took his finger out of the hole and patted her on the stomach. It was then that he felt the unmistakable shape of a condom packet in a little pocket tucked inside her shorts.

"You are so gonna be punished for this," he said.

Cami smiled at her new lover, knowing somehow it wouldn't be quite that way.

ABOUT THE AUTHORS

BONNIE DEE is an erotica and erotic romance writer with numerous novels published at Liquid Silver Books, Venus Press and Samhain Publishing. Her short stories have been included in *Best Women's Erotica 2006* and *Wicked Words: Sex at the Sports Club*. For more information on the author and her backlist of books go to bonniedee.com.

A. D. R. FORTE's erotic short fiction has appeared in the anthologies *Awakening the Virgin 2, Lips Like Sugar* (Cleis Press), and in *Scared Naked Magazine*. She lives in Texas and tries to avoid daylight hours as much as possible.

B. J. FRANKLIN has only been writing erotica for a short while. Her first published story "The Wheels on the Bus" appears at GoodVibes.com, and she has two stories in print: "The Lady-killer" is in Sage Vivant and M. Christian's *Amazons* anthology, and "The Power of Imagination" is in Violet Blue's *Lips Like*

Sugar anthology. She is a member of the Erotica Readers and Writers Association, a Trekkie and, in her spare time, studies medicine at university.

Decadent, devilish and delightful are three words that have been used to describe the work of **K. L. GILLESPIE.** She wrote her first story, about a child-eating nun, at age seven, and since then she has worked as a music journalist, art gallery curator and screenwriter. She is a regular contributor to *TANK* magazine and has recently been published in *Wicked: Sexy Tales of Legendary Lovers, Best Women's Erotica 2006, Dying for It: Stories of Sex and Death* and *The Mammoth Book of Erotica.* Her eagerly anticipated first novel, *Jesus Loves Penge* is out later this year.

MARIA GRIGORIADIS lives in Boston, MA and works as a researcher for a biotechnology company in Cambridge conducting research on cancer therapeutics. She is currently working toward a masters in Biotechnology and holds a first degree black belt in Tae Kwon Do. When she is not doing all this, or writing erotica, she plays flag football in an all women's (lesbian) league.

REEN GUIERRE likes sex with a twist. Her steamy stories always end with a little surprise. Her characters—far from being perfect—encounter the unexpected, experience uncertainty and make mistakes, but in spite of it all, still manage to have great sex. She lives with her partner in the frozen north where staying warm on a winter's night is as paramount as the pines. Reen's stories have appeared in *Best Women's Erotica 2007,* Goodvibes.com, and *Oysters and Chocolate.* Contact her at reenguierre@yahoo.com.

DEBRA HYDE's fiction has appeared in several anthologies, most recently *Erotic Travel Tales 2, Best of the Best Meat Erotica* and *Ripe Fruit: Erotica for Well-Seasoned Lovers,* with additional work scheduled to appear in several upcoming anthologies. She is a regular contributor to both Scarlet Letters (www.scarletletters.com) and Yes Portal (www.yesportal.com), and maintains the pansexual blog, Pursed Lips.

KAY JAYBEE currently resides in the southwest of England where she can usually be found in any number of coffee shops. She has had several stories and poems placed on the erotic site OystersandChocolate.com, along with short stories in both *Lips Like Sugar* (Cleis Press), and *Sex and Music* (Black Lace).

GENEVA KING (genevaking.com) has stories appearing in several anthologies including *Ultimate Lesbian Erotica 2006, Best Women's Erotica 2006, Ultimate Undies, Caramel Flava* and *Travelrotica for Lesbians.* She intends to publish a book, if her professors ever give her enough time to do so.

MARIA MATTHEWS is an erotic fiction writer cleverly disguised as a university professor. She lives in the Midwest with her two partners, two kids, one cat, and too much to do. This is her first published erotic short story.

JEAN ROBERTA teaches English at a Canadian university and writes in several genres. Her nonfiction has appeared in *Harrington Lesbian Literary Quarterly* as well as *Perceptions,* a GLBT newsmagazine of the northern prairie. Her erotic fiction has appeared in over fifty print anthologies on both sides of the Atlantic, including *Best Women's Erotica 2000, 2003, 2005* and *2006* and *Best New Erotica 6.*

TERESA NOELLE ROBERTS writes erotica, poetry, romance, and speculative fiction. Her erotica has appeared in *Best Women's Erotica 2004, 2005* and *2007; Secret Slaves: Erotic Stories of Bondage;* FishNetMag; and many other publications. She is also one-half of the erotica-writing duo Sophie Mouette, whose novel *Cat Scratch Fever* was released in 2006 by Black Lace Books. When not writing or copyediting, she can often be found belly dancing or enjoying the beach.

SUSAN ST. AUBIN's erotic writing has been published over the past twenty years in various journals and anthologies, such as *Yellow Silk, Herotica, Best Lesbian Erotica 2001, Ripe Fruit: Erotica for Well-Seasoned Lovers, Best Women's Erotica 2004, The Best of Both Worlds: Bisexual Erotica, Transfigures: Transgender Erotica,* and *Best American Erotica 2007.* She lives in the San Francisco Bay Area.

SLOANE SQUARE has been writing adult microfiction for over a decade. She spends her days and nights soaking in the sights, sounds and smells of human interaction in the big city. She could be sitting next to you on the subway. Or eavesdropping on your conversation at the bar. Her weekly podcast can be enjoyed at nexttuesday.net.

SASKIA WALKER (saskiawalker.co.uk) is a British author who has had erotic fiction published on both sides of the pond. You can find her work in many anthologies including *Best Women's Erotica 2006, Red Hot Erotica, Slave to Love, Secrets Volume 15, The Mammoth Book of Best New Erotica Volume 5,* and *Stirring Up a Storm.* Her longer work includes the novella *Sex, Lies, and Bondage Tape,* and the novels *Along for the Ride* and *Double Dare.*

KRISTINA WRIGHT is a full-time writer whose erotic fiction has appeared in over thirty anthologies, including four editions of the Lambda Award–winning series *Best Lesbian Erotica;* two editions of *Best Women's Erotica;* two volumes of the *Mammoth Book of Best New Erotica* and three editions of *Ultimate Lesbian Erotica.* Her work has also been featured in the nonfiction guide *The Many Joys of Sex Toys* and in e-zines such as Clean Sheets, Scarlet Letters and Good Vibes Magazine. Kristina holds a BA in English and an MA in humanities. For more information about her life, writing and academic pursuits, visit her website kristinawright.com.

ANDREA ZANIN thinks about sex all the time. She's a Montreal-based alternative sexuality educator, and is active in the queer, polyamory and BDSM communities as well as being a trans ally. She writes on topics related to queer, poly and kinky sexuality for a variety of print and online publications as well as being a prolific blogger. Andrea has been writing erotic fiction since she was a teenager, but has only recently come out of the closet with it. She can be found online at sexgeek.ca.

ABOUT THE EDITOR

VIOLET BLUE is the best-selling, award-winning author and editor of nearly two dozen books on sex and sexuality, all currently in print, three of which have been translated into languages including French, Spanish and Russian. Violet is a sex educator who lectures at University of Callifornia branches and community teaching institutions, and writes about erotica, pornography, sexual pleasure and health. She is a professional sex blogger and femmebot; the sex columnist for the *San Francisco Chronicle;* a Geek Entertainment TV correspondent, an author at Metroblogging San Francisco; and is on the Gawker Media payroll at Fleshbot.com. She is a San Francisco native and human blog; she lists her profession as "wetware hacker" and her sexual orientation as binary. She has survived being a Dorkbot presenter twice and over ten years at Survival Research Laboratories, and is a notorious podcaster and videoblogger. Her podcast Open Source Sex has made iTunes cry for its mommy at least once. She has been interviewed, featured, and quoted as an expert by more magazine, web, television and radio outlets than can be listed here, including Boing Boing, the *Wall Street Journal, Newsweek,* NPR, *O: The Oprah Magazine,* MSNBC, CNN, *Wired, Esquire* and Web MD; for more information visit her websites tinynibbles.com and techyum.com, or listen to her podcast, Open Source Sex.